Christmas at the
Edge of the World

Christmas at the Edge of the World

Kate Hewitt

TULE
PUBLISHING

Chapter One

"I'M SORRY. WE do try to be as understanding as possible in these types of situations, but I am afraid in this instance Zachary's behaviour is completely unacceptable." The headmaster's face was drawn into stern lines of displeasure tempered by very little sympathy. "I have no choice but to exclude Zachary permanently from the school."

Laurel's stomach plunged unpleasantly at this news even as she wondered how to react to it. She wasn't sure whether she should nod in agreement or tell the man what he could do with his so-called understanding. She did neither, re-crossing her legs as she shot her nephew an uncertain, questioning look. Shouldn't he be contributing to this awful, awkward conversation?

He hadn't said a word since she'd been summoned to the prestigious St. Luke's School for Boys fifteen minutes ago, after being told the situation was both urgent and serious. Laurel had a lot of both urgent and serious in the last ten days, enough to last her a lifetime, and yet here was more.

"I'm sure Zac is aware of the…the severity of his behaviour," she said after a moment, because she had to say something, and in truth, she wasn't sure what it should be.

Should she let this obnoxious man with his sniffy attitude and stupid bow tie walk all over her, as well as her nephew?

Perhaps not, but neither could she pretend Zac hadn't acted anything but outrageously and, in this case, dangerously. He deserved what he was getting. Unfortunately.

At fourteen years old going on about forty, Zac looked indifferent to the pronouncement that he would no longer be able to attend the school where he'd been going since he'd been in year three. He was sprawled in a chair, inspecting his nails, his school tie bunched in one pocket, working hard at looking completely unconcerned.

Laurel had become used to that look; it had been his standard since she'd taken over his care. Even now, ten days on, she fought a sense of unreality that she was here, that this man-child was her responsibility, at least for the next three weeks. With every passing day, that responsibility had felt more daunting, more impossible.

And now, with Zac's exclusion from school, the latest in a depressingly long line of offences, she was starting to wonder if this *was* impossible. If she just couldn't do it, no matter how hard she hoped or tried, or what her best intentions had been when her sister Abby had checked herself into a four-week private rehab facility a little more than a week ago.

Utterly out of the blue, Laurel had received a phone call from a staff member at the facility, informing her that Abby had asked her to take care of Zac, the nephew she'd seen, at most, a handful of times since he'd been born.

"But what's happened? Where is she? Is Abby okay?" The

questions had bubbled out of Laurel like lava, but the staff member had refused to give anything away.

"She is in a private facility," she'd said repressively, while Laurel's mind had spun emptily. She hadn't known her sister had been battling some kind of addiction, if that was even what the problem was. She hadn't known much about her sister at all, because Abby had walked away from her and their family life over twenty years ago, and Laurel could count the number of times she'd seen her since then on one hand. Not including her thumb.

Now, with this sudden request to take care of the nephew she'd seen sporadically over the years, she had no idea what to do, or how to feel.

"Take *care* of him…" she'd repeated dumbly, a cup of tea cooling by her elbow, her laptop screen on the current batch of edits of a medical journal, and her cat Mistral curled up in her lap. Outside the window of her study, York Minster's majestic Gothic spires pierced a wintry sky. "You mean, in London?"

"She's left instructions at her flat and a key with the doorman," the staff member had replied neutrally. "She said you would be amenable."

Amenable? That felt rich, coming from a sister who had chosen to cut herself out of Laurel's life as if she were wielding a particularly sharp pair of scissors. And yet of course Laurel was amenable, because no matter how Abby had walked away, or how much it had hurt, she'd been there when it had mattered. Even though they'd become more or less estranged for all of Laurel's adulthood, she owed Abby her life, or at least her childhood.

Her job as a freelance copyeditor meant she could work from anywhere, and things were slow around Christmas as it was. And so Laurel had dropped everything to come to London to look after Zac, picking him up from school to both their bewilderment; he barely knew who she was, and she'd had to ask a teacher to point him out. Awkward didn't even begin to cover it.

And yet, despite all that, Laurel had been buoyed by an indefatigable optimism that had been the touchstone of her life. Admittedly, some of her friends had pointed out, kindly, that her optimism was more naiveté than anything else, and others had told her that expecting a hero worthy of a Jane Austen adaptation wasn't optimism, but delusion, and yet…

Laurel kept wanting to believe life worked out in the end, that there was a reason bad things happened, that silver linings existed even when she hadn't found them yet. That it was all ahead of her, all still going to happen. The miracle. The magic. Not just with finding Mr Right, but with everything. With this.

And so, like with everything else, she'd held onto that hope with Zac. Unfortunately, he had not shared her optimism.

The initial awkwardness she had understandably anticipated hadn't morphed into the friendly let's-get-to-know-each-other sesh that Laurel had been counting on. Her expansive offer of takeaway wasn't seen as a treat but a given; her attempts at conversation had been utterly shut down before she'd barely begun, and a hostility had emanated from

Zac towards her that left her feeling hurt and raw even as she told herself not to take it personally.

Sometimes, when a fourteen-year-old was giving her a glare of death and an eye roll for the twentieth time that *hour*, it was hard not to.

It had all taken Laurel rather miserably by surprise. The last time she'd seen Zac, during a fly-by visit to London a few years ago when Abby had reluctantly agreed to meet up, he'd been a round-faced eleven-year-old, puberty no more than a faint cloud on the horizon. He'd doodled on his placemat and asked her questions about football, and actually listened to her, admittedly ignorant, answers. Still, he'd been sweet.

The gangly six-two stranger her nephew had turned into during the intervening years had completely taken her aback. His voice was deep, his attitude irritable or indifferent in turns, and his fingers appeared to be glued to his phone. Laurel didn't know what to do with any of it. She realised a Happy Meal and a game of Go Fish wasn't going to cut it, not by a long mark.

She still didn't understand why Abby had separated herself from her family as soon as she'd left for university, visits a thing of the past, phone calls and emails eventually going unreturned. Laurel had never worked up the courage to ask her, had felt too hurt and even betrayed to dare to voice it out loud, afraid of what the answer might be even as she knew no answer would satisfy, no reason would be good enough to justify her sister's behaviour.

Anyway, back at the beginning, she'd been able to convince herself it wasn't as bad as it had felt; Abby was busy, she'd come home at Christmas, she had answered that email, even if it was only one line. *Don't be so sensitive*, Laurel had told herself, but eventually that kind of optimistic talking-to wore thin, and been replaced with both confusion and a deep, abiding hurt that Laurel told herself she'd got past a long time ago.

At least, after Zac had been born, as far as Laurel could tell with no father in the picture, Abby had grudgingly agreed to see Laurel a couple of times, but the visits had been few and far between, a stilted lunch and one afternoon in Hamley's, with Laurel fobbing off the confusion and sorrow she felt with an overpriced teddy bear that Zac had hurled to the ground.

So it happened that now, as she swanned into London to save the day, she didn't actually *know* her nephew, or even her sister, or what their lives were like, or what they might be struggling with. Yet here she was, trying to do the best she could, wanting it to work out, to somehow magic a happy ending out of a situation that felt awkward and desperate and sad.

Here *they* were, she acknowledged, dealing with yet another of Zac's misdemeanours—he'd had three in the last week and a half—although this time his behaviour seemed to have veered into alarming felony territory.

"Whether Zac is aware of the severity of his behaviour is of no concern to me," the headmaster stated with asperity, all pretence of sympathy well and truly vanished. He straightened in his chair, everything about him bristling and indignant. "He has had three warnings, and as of today, he is no longer a pupil at this institution."

Well. There wasn't much she could say to that, was there? Laurel glanced again at Zac, who let out a bored sigh, as if this were all so very tedious, so his artfully-gelled shaggy blond fringe blew upwards. She gritted her teeth, telling herself not to be irritated by his behaviour, as he undoubtedly wanted her to be. She'd had her patience tested far too much in the last ten days, and she felt it fraying thread by fragile thread. Her initial desire to create some sort of happy reunion with her nephew had fizzled into merely surviving the encounter, and now, sitting in this stuffy office, she just longed to go home.

She wanted nothing more than to return to the cosy safety of her little terraced cottage in York, her small circle of friends, her lovable grey cat, Mistral. Cups of tea with her elderly neighbour Helen, an evening of Netflix, with Jane Austen adaptions featuring heavily, and dreams of the perfect man to sustain her—Gilbert Blythe with a dash of Mr Darcy, because she knew he was out there, somewhere. He'd be tall and dark and brooding, slightly mysterious but with a hidden gentleness that only she could see. All right, maybe not *quite* like that, but he'd be a hero, *her* hero, a knight in shining armour, and the boy next door all rolled into one.

That old life felt very far away as the headmaster cleared his throat, waiting for Laurel to make the next move. Unfortunately, she had no idea what it was. Would Abby have fought this? Would she have threatened the headmaster with litigation, or at least a sternly-worded letter to the board of governors? Or would she have made Zac apologise and pay for the damage?

Laurel had no clue. She hadn't had a proper conversation with her sister in well over five years, and in any case, she had little experience of managing children. She was thirty-six, single, and childless; her only experience of kids was avoiding the stroppy ones in the supermarket.

Not that she *disliked* children; she'd dreamed about having one someday, although admittedly that possibility was becoming more and more remote.

Some of her friends had babies, and she'd had a few cuddles, although she tended to hand them back when they became slobbery or sticky, or started to cry. Older children were cute in theory, but they scared her a bit, and they were alien, just as Zac was, with his sullen silences, his difficult behaviour, his cracked veneer of bored indifference, with a sudden rage sometimes shining through that both alarmed and moved her, because part of her understood it, at least a bit.

His mother had just checked herself into rehab, without, it seemed, any warning. Laurel didn't know what their relationship had been before that but judging by the circumstances as well as Zac's behaviour she had a feeling it hadn't been stellar.

"I think there's nothing more to be said, then," she said finally, with a useless attempt at dignity, and rose from her chair. "Zac?"

Heaving another bored sigh, Zac unfolded his lanky form from his chair and strode out of the room without looking at his former headmaster or his aunt.

A few minutes later, they were standing outside the school's venerable doors in Wimbledon, an arctic wind cutting through Laurel's jumper; she'd forgotten to put on a coat when she'd received the phone call from the headmaster's PA to come immediately.

She shivered as she clicked the key fob to unlock her sister's behemoth of a shiny black Rover, all gleaming chrome and supple leather, with a smell of air freshener and not so much as a crumb or a candy wrapper to sully its pristine surfaces. Zac threw himself into the front seat and slid out his phone, his head angled away from Laurel.

Now what? It was just a little over a week till Christmas, and Abby wasn't meant to receive visitors until January, a full four weeks after she'd checked herself in.

When Laurel had called the rehab facility—a place, she saw online, that cost nearly a thousand pounds a night— they'd practically scolded her.

"Miss Dalton requests no contact until her period of treatment is over."

"But I'm taking care of her son," Laurel had said in exasperation. "Doesn't she care about that?"

"I believe she's made all the necessary arrangements, but if you feel incapable of caring for him, then perhaps we need to ring—"

"No, never mind," Laurel had said hastily. The last thing she wanted to do was get child protection services involved. "I just wanted some information." Which she hadn't received, naturally.

"Well?" she asked Zac now. "Do you have anything to say about all this?"

Shrug. *Of course.*

Laurel took a deep breath as she rested her hands on the steering wheel. "You set fire to the chemistry lab, Zac?" she stated, a faint question mark in her tone; the headmaster had informed her of his crime before she'd so much as sat down, but it still seemed unbelievable, even for Zac.

Another shrug. "We were just messing around."

"You could have put someone in serious danger, or worse. You could have been charged with a *crime*—" Thankfully, the school, as well as the harried teacher who had put out the fire, had chosen not to press any charges.

Zac blew out another breath, this time one of annoyance. "It was a joke."

"Some joke." Laurel shook her head, knowing she was hitting all the wrong notes with her nephew, as she seemed to have done since she'd come to London. She'd been intending to try so hard, and at first she had, but this was one situation where a smile and a determined attitude just wasn't going to work. But what was?

Briefly Laurel closed her eyes. *I can't do this.* She'd been trying not to say that since the beginning, but the drumbeat of defeat inside her head was becoming louder and louder. *I can't do this. I really can't do this.*

And yet she had to, because what other choice was there? She only had two and a half weeks to go. Even if she felt like a failure for not bonding with her nephew, she'd still manage to keep him fed, clothed, and alive. *Hopefully.* Maybe that was all she could expect from this situation…even if it made her feel like a failure, and worse, it made her feel sad. She wanted more for Zac. She wanted more for her relationship with him.

Although, Laurel reflected rather grimly, she could hardly swan off the second Abby came out of rehab, *if* she came out of rehab then, although perhaps Abby would want her to go. She'd certainly never seemed to want her around, in the last twenty-odd years. Laurel pushed away that bitter thought, because the last thing she needed right now was to remember all that old hurt.

Right now, she had to focus on Zac. She just wished she could manage it better, that they could get along instead of all this sullen silence and hostility, punctuated by sneers, insults, and eye rolls. And what was she supposed to do about his education? School broke up this week for Christmas, so at least she didn't have to think about it until after the new year, and Abby would be back soon after that. Maybe she wouldn't have to deal with it at all.

With a sigh, Laurel started the car and began navigating it out of the school car park, while Zac sat oblivious next to her, absorbed in his phone.

That was another thing she had no idea about, Laurel reflected as she drove the massive SUV down London's streets, wincing every time a car veered too close. Phones. Did Zac have screen time rules? Should she take his phone away at night? She'd suggested it, rather tentatively, the first night, and Zac hadn't even deigned to reply. Laurel had left it, as she had so many other things to deal with.

The trouble was, she thought, far from the first time, was that she had no sense of authority with her nephew; they'd had no relationship before ten days ago, and they still had no relationship as far as she could tell, despite her initial, admittedly rather paltry, efforts.

Besides that, she had no idea how long this whole surreal limbo was going to last. In a little less than three weeks, would Abby stroll back into her flat and take up her life as if she had been on an extended holiday? Laurel didn't know, because she didn't know *Abby*.

From sleeping in the same bed and plaiting each other's hair—well, Abby plaiting hers, at least—they'd become these strangers who could barely manage to keep the chitchat going for half an hour, and who both felt a treacherous relief when they said goodbye.

It saddened Laurel too much to think about it, and so she generally didn't…which meant she'd stopped trying with Abby a while ago, and the visits and phone calls, already sporadic, had become more and more infrequent as well as strained.

Laurel pulled into the underground car park of the high-end luxury building where her sister had a glamorous, if rather sterile, flat in South London. Laurel hated its bland, empty rooms, the cream leather furniture all looking like it shouldn't ever be touched never mind sat on, the highlights of chrome and glass so stark and unfriendly.

She didn't know how her sister had managed to raise a child in that place, although there was very little evidence that she actually had. No toys, no photos, no crayoned pictures on the fridge, although admittedly Zac was fourteen and not five, so perhaps the days of homemade drawings were long gone. Judging by her nephew's current behaviour, they most certainly were.

Still, it was a far cry from Laurel's cosy terraced cottage back in York, crammed with junk she liked to think of as antiques, the overstuffed sofa covered with colourful knitted throws, the walls lined with paintings she picked up in charity shops and car boot sales.

With a pang, Laurel pushed away thoughts of the home she missed with a fierce ache. She'd asked Helen to water her plants and take care of her cat. Helen had been most obliging, and sent Laurel away with assurances that everything would be looked after, and she knew it would be. She just wanted to be the one to look after it.

She wanted to be *home*, not in this awful, elegant flat with a fourteen-year-old boy who acted as if he either hated or couldn't care less about her, and who, Laurel thought now, was capable of setting a room on fire. *No joke.*

To spend Christmas, her absolutely favourite time of year, in such a place felt awful, impossible. She didn't want to do it. She *couldn't*.

"Zac, this can't go on." She hadn't realised the words were out of her mouth until she said them, standing in her sister's sleek galley kitchen while Zac walked away from her towards her bedroom, eyes glued to his iPhone's screen. He kept walking as if she hadn't spoken. "*Zac.*"

Still nothing. After ten days of this kind of behaviour, Laurel was used to it, but for once she had no more patience or understanding to draw on, and she strode forward, clamping one hand on his shoulder. "Zac, *listen* to me."

He jerked away from her, causing her hand to fly up, and she took a stumbling step backward, staring at him in surprise even though she supposed, considering his actions today, she shouldn't be.

"Zac," she said again, trying to keep her voice even, "this can't go on."

He rolled his eyes. "So, go."

"Go?" She stared at him in confusion. "I'm not *going.*"

"I don't care if you do."

The snarl sounded genuine, but Laurel reminded herself of the uncertainty that surely had to lie beneath it. "I know that," she said as patiently as she could. "Trust me, but that's not the answer here. I'm trying to help…"

"Whatever."

Deep breath. Reminder that Zac had a right to be angry, and she was big enough not to take it personally. "Look," she said, trying to sound both friendly and practical, "we have nearly three more weeks before your mum comes home, and I don't want to struggle through them all, especially at Christmas—"

"I don't care about Christmas."

Which made her feel sad, because Laurel loved Christmas. And York was magical at Christmas, with the lights strung through the narrow, medieval streets, the Christmas fairs and markets, the big, bushy tree she got every year and the homemade decorations…for a second, Laurel considered going back to York. She had a spare bedroom; she and Zac could stay there until Abby returned. But even as she thought about it, she knew it wouldn't work.

Her house was absolutely tiny and crammed with precious junk; Zac would knock into things every time he turned around. In any case, the problems she was facing with Zac would be just as present in York as they were in London—the hostility, his phone, the feeling that she couldn't do anything right.

Yet she meant what she said. This couldn't go on. She couldn't let it. Something had to change.

"Look, I'm sorry I got excluded, okay?" Zac said, surprising her. "I hated that snobby school anyway. But don't worry, I'll stay out of your way." His lip curled in a sneer as he raised his eyebrows. "So it's cool, right?"

"No, it's not *cool*. And that's not what I meant." She stared at him in growing frustration. "Can't we please just…" *Get along?* She swallowed down the words, knowing they weren't the right ones. Unfortunately, she had no idea which ones were. "I want things to be better," she said a bit desperately, and Zac just rolled his eyes. Again.

Laurel watched him saunter to his room and slam the door, feeling completely powerless as well as out of her depth. Three more weeks. But *Christmas…*

She thought about ringing her dad up in Yorkshire, maybe even going up there for a visit, but she knew that wouldn't work either. Her father had retired from the police force five years ago, and he took a dim view of any kind of misbehaviour, especially surly boys he'd class as juvenile delinquents.

Besides, he hadn't spoken to Abby since before Zac's birth, and he'd never even met his grandson, something Laurel didn't understand but had accepted as just the way it—and he—was. Tom West was an old-school kind of father; he'd never been hands-on, never said much at all, but she'd always known he loved her. Still, Laurel didn't think now was the time for a family reunion.

And yet the thought of staying in this modern flat, all sleek surfaces and high-tech gadgets, where she knew no one, and where Christmas couldn't happen, made her want to scream. She couldn't spend the holidays here. She needed to get away, and so did Zac, find some kind of fresh start, even if it was only a temporary one.

But where? Where could they go that was both comforting and different, preferably without phone signal or even Wi-Fi, somewhere they could actually get to know one another and leave all this aggro behind? Assuming they even wanted to get to know one another, which Laurel wasn't sure she did, never mind Zac.

But, still. A second chance, even if just for a little while. A break, of sorts, for them both, while they waited out Abby's treatment. *A silver lining.*

The answer, when it came, seemed so obvious Laurel was surprised she hadn't thought of it before. Of course, she hadn't been there since she'd been eight years old, so it was understandable that it didn't spring immediately to mind. But it was lovely and welcoming and there was *definitely* no phone signal.

Orkney.

The word alone conjured up all sorts of images—midnight walks on the beach, as the sun finally began to set, and rainy afternoons by the fire playing Ludo and Chinese chequers. The salty sting of the wind, the air so fresh she could feel it fill her lungs, cleaning her from the inside out. Biking down narrow lanes, drippy ice cream cones by the harbour side, gulls wheeling and crying overhead, playing cards at the tiny table in Bayview Cottage's window...*magic*. All of it magic.

Before she could think about all the pros and the inevitable, undoubted cons, Laurel grabbed her phone and scrolled through her contacts, pressing the number for her Great-Aunt Eilidh, praying that she'd pick up, and more importantly, that she'd welcome two very unexpected guests for Christmas at this late date.

"Laurel? How lovely for you to ring." Her great-aunt's voice was as warm and welcoming as ever, filled with genuine delight at hearing from her. It had been too long, Laurel knew. It always was.

When had she last seen her aunt? Two or three years ago, at least, when Eilidh had come for a weekend in York, and before that it had probably been even longer.

"I'm afraid I'm ringing to ask you a favour," Laurel said in apology. "A rather desperate one."

"If I can help, I will."

Her aunt's certain tone made Laurel's eyes sting. Aunt Eilidh had been lovely when she'd been younger, always welcoming her and Abby to her tiny stone cottage on the windswept island of Orkney off the north coast of Scotland.

Laurel's mum Isla used to bring them there in the summer, two long, lazy, wonderful weeks of doing nothing much and loving every minute. Her mother had loved it too; Laurel remembered her saying they were her favourite two weeks of the year.

One summer, it had rained every day for the entire two weeks, and yet it had still felt magical. Tucked up by the fireplace in Eilidh's cosy sitting room, with mugs of hot cocoa and endless card games...there had been no other place Laurel had wanted to be.

It had all ended when Laurel's mum had died when she'd been just eight. Cervical cancer, just six weeks from diagnosis to death. Her father had never been to Orkney, even though Isla grew up there, and he hadn't wanted to go then, or ever.

Eilidh had come to Scarborough to visit them a few times, but those visits had tapered off in Laurel's teen years, and somehow Laurel had never made it all the way up to Orkney again, even though she'd always said she would, and had told herself to plan a trip one day soon. Somehow it had never happened.

But she wanted to go now.

"What do you need, Laurel?" Eilidh asked gently.

"I want to invite myself for Christmas," Laurel said in an embarrassed rush. "Zac and me...I don't even know if you've met Zac..."

"Abby's son," Eilidh said quietly. "Only once, when he was a baby."

"I'm taking care of him for a bit, which I can explain later, but...we need a break from, well, from real life, I suppose. And I thought of your cottage in Orkney…I have such wonderful memories from there." A sudden thought occurred to her. "You do still have it, don't you? I don't even know…" She was ashamed to admit the depth of her ignorance. Maybe Eilidh had sold it years ago, and never told her.

"Yes, I still have it," Eilidh said with a smile in her voice. "But I'm afraid I'm not there right now. I'm spending the winter in Spain…my joints, you know. I'm not as young as I once was."

"Oh…" Disappointment swamped her, tasting thick and sour in her mouth. "It was a long shot," Laurel said, trying to keep her voice from wobbling. She was feeling rather ridiculously bereft, considering how sudden and mad her idea had been. Going to Orkney wouldn't have been some sort of cure-all, anyway. "I shouldn't have even…"

"There's no reason why you and Zac can't go on your own," Eilidh interjected. "If you want to. I know it might not be quite the same, but the place is empty, and the key is under the flower pot. You're welcome to stay for as long as you like. I won't be back until February."

"Oh…" Eilidh made it sound so simple. Just get in the car and go. Yet Orkney had to be over seven hundred miles from London, plus the ferry…it would take well over twelve hours to get there. It really had been a mad idea.

"Just let me know," Eilidh continued. "And I'll make sure my neighbour Archie MacDougall looks out for you. He minds the place while I'm gone. I can send him an email tonight."

"Are you sure…"

"It's as simple as that."

"Right." Laurel's mind spun. She couldn't really hare off to Orkney Island for Christmas, could she, no matter what she'd been thinking a few moments ago, when the thought of Eilidh's cosy welcome had loomed, bright and hopeful, a mumsy figure for both her and Zac, someone to take care of everything?

What if Abby needed to get in touch? What if she *minded*? What if Zac refused?

And yet…Orkney. A memory of sitting curled up in front of Eilidh's fire while the sun set over the beach outside, sending golden rays slanting through the sashed window…feeling entirely at peace, as if all was right with the world. Knowing there was nowhere else she'd rather be.

"Let me work on a few things here," Laurel said impulsively. "And then I'll ring you back. Thank you so much for the offer, Aunt Eilidh. You're brilliant."

"It's my pleasure, Laurel," Eilidh answered, a trace of sorrow in her voice. "I hope you always know that."

"I do," Laurel answered, and she heard the same sorrow in her voice too, like a whisper from the past. She wished she'd kept in better touch with her aunt over the years. She wished her father had taken them to Orkney when they were children, and those magical summers had continued, stretching on to a golden horizon, shared memories that might have knit her and Abby, Eilidh, and her father, together all those years ago.

But he hadn't, and they hadn't, and here they were, all of

them separate and isolated in their own ways.

"Thank you for the offer," Laurel said, meaning every word. "Let me see if I can make it happen."

Chapter Two

"THIS IS *IT*?"

Zac's lip curled as he stared out at the twinkling lights of the tiny town of Stromness, obscured both by both darkness and a steadily falling rain as the ferry pulled into the choppy harbour.

Laurel's stomach had been roiling since they'd got on the boat over an hour ago; ferry crossings in the North Sea in December were not, she'd realised, altogether advisable. She'd nearly lost her lunch more than once, and a cold sweat dotted her hairline and prickled between her shoulder blades as she said a silent prayer of thanks that the wretched ferry trip was nearly over.

"Yes, this is it," she managed, trying desperately to inject a cheerful note into her voice despite her churning stomach. "Aunt Eilidh's cottage is right on the coast, with a garden that leads straight onto the beach. It's amazing."

Of course, at half past eight at night in the middle of winter, it was also pitch dark and freezing cold. Somehow, when she'd been painting her magical picture of Orkney for Zac's dubious benefit, Laurel had forgotten that they would be here in the dead of winter, rather than the endless, hazy days of July. A man on the ferry had cheerfully informed them that at this, the darkest time of the year, the island enjoyed just six hours of daylight. It was a bleak thought.

Zac had been nonplussed, to say the least, when Laurel had rather airily informed him last night that they were heading to Orkney for Christmas.

"Where?" He'd stared at her incredulously while Laurel had wittered on determinedly.

"My great-aunt's cottage, in the north of Scotland. Your great-great-aunt's, you know. She's lovely." And she wouldn't be there. "It's a wonderful place, full of charm." As if fourteen-year-old boys cared about charm. "I thought we could use a change of scenery," Laurel finished a bit desperately, and to her surprise, Zac had stared at her for a long moment and then merely shrugged.

"Fine. Whatever," he said, and walked off.

Laurel decided to take it as a win. She wasn't going to have to drag him there kicking and screaming, at least, and once they got to Eilidh's cottage...well, things would get better. A lot better. They would start to make sense. Or so she was desperately hoping—that the magic of Eilidh's cottage was still there, still worked.

Now, after nine hours of driving through Christmas traffic and the hour-long ferry from Scrabster, Laurel was still clinging onto that hope, more out of sheer, bloody-minded determination than actual belief, but still. Good things were going to happen.

Zac had barely spoken to her all day, immersed as usual in his phone, although the signal had become patchy on the ferry, and he'd resorted to staring moodily out at the darkened sea instead. Conversation was clearly not an option, and Laurel decided to wait until they were settled in the cottage, cosy and warm, before she attempted to crack his cold veneer.

The ship began to creak and clank like Marley's ghost as it drew up to the quay, and Laurel climbed back into the Rover. "The cottage is only a few minutes away," she said brightly. "Right on the beach. We'll be there in no time."

Zac did not reply. What a surprise.

Soon they were driving off the boat into Stromness, a town Laurel remembered as quaint and charming, with steep, narrow streets, some of them cobbled, and terraced cottages rising above on the hillside. She couldn't see any of it in the impenetrable darkness of a midwinter's night, and as she followed the traffic off the ferry, she wished she'd thought to print out some directions to Bayview Cottage.

For some inexplicable reason, she'd thought she'd be able to find her way instinctively—take a right off the boat, follow the street to the edge of town, the cottage was on the right. She remembered her mother calling back to them, saying how they were almost there, as she and Abby pressed their noses to the back window and watched the town's main street wind its way along the harbour, thrilled to be back on the island and soon out of the car.

Only everything looked different now; there was even a Tesco Superstore in Kirkwall, Laurel had seen online, and Stromness seemed bigger too, more buildings along the narrow harbour side street, ones she didn't recognise or remember, and had the street really been this *long*? In her memory it had been a few seconds between the ferry and Bayview, but clearly that hadn't been the case.

"I thought you said it was only a few minutes away?" Zac said, startling her because she'd half-forgotten he was there. She was hunched over the steering wheel, peering at the road, her eyes straining in the darkness, the car's headlights seeming to make very little difference against the impenetrable blackness that loomed everywhere.

"It is."

"We've been driving for ten minutes."

"Have we? Goodness." The buildings had dropped off so all was darkness, the water no more than a black gleam in the distance, more a sense than a reality. "I suppose I missed it. It's been awhile since I've been here." Zac sighed heavily. And biting her lip, Laurel manoeuvred the huge Rover into a dirt track in her best attempt at a three-point turn. It was closer to seven.

"It should be up here on the left somewhere..." Laurel murmured as she headed back towards town, hanging onto her upbeat tone by a thread. "I know it's right on the edge of Stromness..." Although was it? She and Abby had walked into town, but it had taken ages. Laurel remembered complaining that her feet hurt. So maybe it wasn't as close as her hazy memory had made her believe. Maybe nothing was as she'd remembered, a possibility that made her stomach lurch in panic.

And why was it so *dark*? It had never been dark when they'd driven up before, but then, of course, it had been summer, the season of midnight sunsets, rooms full of golden light even as she'd been going to sleep. It certainly wasn't like that now.

"*Where?*" Zac demanded. There was nothing to see anywhere but field and sea and darkness. Lots of darkness.

"Somewhere…" Laurel bit her lip. She'd been really stupid not to look the directions up on Google, and of course her phone had no signal, something she'd actually been grateful for, except for now when she could most definitely use it. And the truth was she'd had some naïve, fairy-tale belief that everything would magically fall into place the second she arrived on the island, because this was Orkney, land that she loved. Right.

Just then, with the world feeling so unfamiliar and so dark, Laurel's optimism slipped. She almost wished they hadn't come. What if the cottage wasn't the cure-all she was naively hoping it could be? Or if not a cure-all, then at least some sort of beginning, a way to make this right, or at least better. Surely that wasn't too much to hope for?

"What does it even look like?" Zac asked.

"It's a little stone cottage, right by the sea. It's got a steep slate roof and a little blue gate in front…" And that was all Laurel could remember, actually. But here was an unexpected plus—she and Zac were having more conversation now than they'd had in the last eleven days. "It's lovely," she finished, a bit lamely, as Zac peered out the window.

"Is that it?" He flung out a hand towards a narrow lane leading off to the left, a building barely visible in the distance, behind some runty looking trees and a tall, prickly hedge.

"I don't know. I don't remember it being so far from the road." But then she didn't seem to remember much about Bayview Cottage, except for a few hazy details, like some gold-tinted montage from a Disney film. This *was* the right location—somewhere on the outside of Stromness, anyway.

"I suppose we could at least check," Laurel said, and slowly pulled the Rover into the narrow, rutted lane, overgrown hedges brushing either side of the car as they bumped their way towards the cottage.

"There's a gate," Zac said, sounding unimpressed as he nodded towards the house, and Laurel caught sight of a weathered wooden gate hanging off one hinge. Once upon a time it might have been blue.

"Winters are hard here, I suppose," she murmured. At least it looked as if they might be in the right place. Laurel pulled up next to the cottage and turned off the engine. She looked at Zac, who was looking even more unimpressed.

"Are we actually *staying* here?"

"Well, yes. At least, I think we are. Assuming this is Bayview…" Laurel peered at the darkened cottage as she climbed out of the car. "It is!" she called back to Zac. "Look, it says it next to the door." She pointed to a hand-painted slate sign. Zac did not deign to reply.

"It'll be fine inside," Laurel told him bracingly. "And wait till we get the fire going…" She was determined to stay cheerful now, despite the icy wind that blew off the sea, and the rain that needled her face with sharp, stinging points. It was *freezing*. Never mind.

"The key's under the flower pot," she told Zac. "We'll be inside in just a second…"

Except, when she found the cracked, empty flowerpot by the front door, there was no key under it. And there were no other flower pots outside the cottage.

"It's got to be here somewhere…" she said, knowing she was starting to sound desperate. She'd been feeling it about fifteen minutes ago, and soon it was going to turn into full-blown panic. Why was nothing going the way she wanted and needed it to? The way it did in the movies, the way she kept hoping it would turn out?

Zac folded his arms, hunching his shoulders against the rain, wind, and cold. He muttered something under his breath, but Laurel didn't try to make out what it was.

It was all going to be fine. They just needed to get *in* to the place. Then she'd get a fire going, and heat up the stew she'd made last night, chucking every vegetable she could think of into a pot with some barley and broth. And they'd play Ludo…well, perhaps that was stretching credibility a bit. They'd do *something*.

"Maybe it's by the back door," she said, and walked around the cottage in pitch darkness, stumbling over frozen tufts of grass, before she heaved herself over the low stone wall and landed knee-deep in an icy mud puddle. She suppressed a swear word as freezing, dirty water seeped into her boots and onto her jeans, making her feel even colder than she'd already been.

Stumbling through more tufty grass, she made it to the back door, and peered through the smeared and dusty glass to see the darkened shapes of the kitchen she remembered—a small round table up against the window, the two-door Rayburn fit snugly into the old fireplace, the deep farmhouse sink under the other window.

Knowing it was futile, Laurel turned the knob, rattling it uselessly. Of course it was locked. But where was the blasted key? Eilidh had *said* it would be under the flower pot.

There were no flowerpots by the backdoor, nothing but overgrown grass and a nearly threadbare welcome mat. Knowing it was most likely just as futile, Laurel tried the window next to the door. At first it didn't budge a centimetre, but when she gave it another desperate heave, much to her shock, she was able to push the window up a couple of inches as it gave an almighty protesting screech. It sounded as if it hadn't been moved in decades.

Laurel took a deep breath, and pushed again, this time managing to get the window up nearly a foot. Big enough to climb through? It would have to be.

Actually, she decided thirty seconds later, when she'd slung one leg over the ledge, it *wasn't* big enough to climb through. Her back was jammed painfully against the window, making her wince as she straddled the sill, every part of her body protesting at this activity just as the window had when she'd opened it. This was *so* not fun. What if she got stuck? She had a mental image of Zac trying to pry her out of the window and she let out a groan.

"Laurel?" Zac called, a disembodied voice in the darkness. "What's going on?"

"I'm killing myself," Laurel muttered. Death by window,

and one on the ground floor at that. Who would have ever thought? "Just a sec," she called back, unable, in her current position, to inject the usual cheery note in her voice that she feared made her sound a bit manic. Now she just sounded as if she were being strangled. "Be right there…" With a loud *oof* Laurel managed to free herself from the confines of the window, letting out a yelp as her leg stuck on the ledge before she tumbled forward into the kitchen, landing on her knees on the hard, tiled floor. *Ouch.*

At least she was inside. She could unlock the door, she could make a fire…she could…was that a mouse?

As Laurel's eyes adjusted to the darkness, she saw an alarmingly large rodent scuttle behind the Rayburn. The cottage had a forgotten, musty feel; she supposed it had been too much to hope that Eilidh's neighbour would have opened the place up, aired it out, left milk and eggs and even a bottle of wine in the fridge…

No, of course not. This wasn't Airbnb. And it didn't matter anyway, because Laurel had all those things and more in the boot of the car.

"Laurel…" Zac's voice sounded far away, and less bored than it had been in a while. He sounded a little bit worried, bless him.

"Coming," Laurel called as she flicked on the lights, illuminating the small kitchen in a dim and rather sickly glow. She brushed dust and cobwebs from her hair and started towards the front of the cottage. After a bit of fumbling, she managed to unlock the door, letting in a clearly exasperated Zac.

"Seriously?" He gave her a scathingly incredulous look as he looked around the tiny hallway with its faded wallpaper and cracked tile. "This place is a complete *dump*."

Laurel took in the little sitting room with the fireplace that had figured so favourably in her memories, the worn and saggy sofa wedged against one wall, the bookshelf between the window and the fireplace crammed with tattered paperbacks.

All right, it was a lot smaller and, yes, shabbier than she remembered, she could admit that. And the air smelled of damp and dust, and she'd already seen one, possibly two, mice.

But...this was Eilidh's home, and Laurel had always loved it here, just as Abby and her mother had. It had felt...enchanted, somehow. Magical. A place where nothing could go wrong. A place where happiness was a promise.

Perhaps that was why she'd never come back.

Still, once she'd made a fire, and put on some stew, and maybe dusted a little, it would be fine. It would be wonderful, just like it had been before. The magic would work.

"Granted, it's a bit different than you're used to," she told Zac briskly. "But it makes for a nice change."

He shook his head slowly, still so disbelieving, and Laurel decided to ignore him as she turned on a few more lights before heading out to the car for their stuff.

It was still raining steadily, and it looked as if there wasn't a light on in the whole world. The air smelled of brine and coal smoke, and brought back a deluge of misty memories that Laurel couldn't quite hold onto. She missed Eilidh.

She missed her mum. She missed Abby, who would have been right here with her, helping her heft boxes, daring her to race to the freezing sea and be the first to dip her toes in.

All of it made Laurel ache, and she blinked rapidly, banishing the memories because they hurt too much, far more than she'd expected them to. That was why she never let herself think of them. She'd locked them all in a box in the back of her mind and she wasn't ready to take them out now.

What would Abby feel about her taking Zac here? Laurel had left a message at the rehab centre, but as usual she'd received the repressive reply that her sister could not be disturbed. Laurel had wondered at the ethics of taking her nephew so far away, and then had determinedly shrugged it away. In her bones, in her heart, she believed they were in the right place, and at least Abby knew where they were, if she decided to ask.

Back at Eilidh's cottage, she and Zac could get to know one another. Find a way forward. Create a magical Christmas. *Something…*

Or was she completely daft? Naïve bordering on delusional, as her friends liked to laughingly say? *Life doesn't work like that, Laurel.*

But it could, Laurel would say. *It should.*

Suppressing a sigh, she grabbed a box of groceries from the boot of the car and headed back to the house.

Zac was sprawled on the sofa, its rusty springs squeaking under his weight, as he glared at the screen of his phone. "There's no Wi-Fi," he flung at her accusingly.

"No, I don't imagine there would be." Eilidh had never been one for any kind of tech, and even if she had Wi-Fi, Laurel wasn't about to find out how it worked. That was definitely *not* the point of this holiday.

"Are you serious?" Zac demanded. "I didn't expect a signal out here, but no *Wi-Fi*?" He lifted his gaze from his phone to glare at her instead of the screen. "That's, like, child abuse."

"I don't think that would hold in a court of law," Laurel returned as lightly as she could. "And in any case, it might be nice not to have Wi-Fi for a bit. We can do other things."

Zac snorted. "Like what?"

"Board games. Getting ready for Christmas. Walks…" She trailed off, cowed by Zac's sneering look despite her determination to be upbeat. "Why don't you help me get the rest of our stuff from the car?"

Zac opened his mouth to retort something assuredly unsavoury, but then his eyes and mouth both rounded, his face draining of colour. Before Laurel could make a sound, she heard a click behind her. It almost sounded like a gun being cocked, but of course it couldn't be that, that only happened in movies…

Then a low voice, with the thickest Scottish burr Laurel had ever heard, growled at them. "Put your hands up in the air, ye choring skellums."

Chapter Three

H ER HEART POUNDING, Laurel put her hands in the air.
Zac followed, his face sheet-white as his Adam's apple
bobbed in his throat.

Slowly Laurel turned around, bracing herself for whatever Highland lunatic had entered the cottage. Why had she left the door open? Because, of course, she'd thought being in the middle of bloody nowhere meant they were safe. Clearly not.

The man standing in the doorway of the sitting room had a hunting rifle aimed directly at her heart, which was alarming to say the least. He was dressed in indeterminate, mud-splattered clothes—a baggy parka, waterproof plus fours and Wellington boots barely visible beneath a thick layer of caked-on mud. A flat cap was jammed on his head, his craggy face set in a narrowed expression. He looked terrifying—and insane.

"What do you want?" Laurel asked in a shaking voice. "Money? I have some in my wallet…"

"*Money*?" The man's voice was derisive. "It's you who'll be wanting the money, I should think! What are you doing, trying to break in here? Did you think I wouldn't notice?"

It took Laurel a moment to make out his words through his thick Scottish brogue. "We're not breaking in," she protested. "This is my aunt's cottage. And can you please lower that gun before someone gets shot?"

"Your aunt?" The gun didn't move.

"Eilidh Campbell. My great-aunt, actually. The *gun*." Now that she was starting to believe she wasn't in any present or pressing danger, Laurel wanted the hunting rifle taken out of the equation. Slowly she lowered her hands. "We're staying in her cottage over Christmas."

The man lowered the gun a few inches, so Laurel would be shot in the groin rather than the heart if it accidentally— or not so accidentally—went off, which was not a particularly reassuring thought. "Eilidh said naught about it to me."

"Well, trust me, that's the plan. I rang her yesterday and made the arrangements. She's in Spain and she told us the key was under the flowerpot, but it wasn't."

"Oh, aye," the man said, finally, thankfully lowering the gun so neither she nor Zac were in its line of fire. "I'm meant to put the key in the pot for visitors, but she didn't tell aught to me about it." The gun bobbed up again but thankfully was lowered once more.

"You must be her neighbour." Laurel searched her memory for the man's name, and thankfully came up with it. "Archie...MacDougall."

"Aye."

"Well, now you know we're not burglars, and we know you're not some deranged lunatic wandering the coast road." Although, actually, the latter remained to be seen.

"Eilidh tells me when she's having visitors." He still sounded suspicious.

"She said she'd let you know yesterday. Did you get an email?"

Archie frowned. "I don't reckon I checked it last night," he admitted with a crooked smile. "I'm not much of one for technology."

Neither was Eilidh, but at least she had email in Spain. "Well…" Laurel said with a shrug, because what else could she do?

Archie gave a grudging nod. "Right, I suppose you're deserving of an apology." Laurel waited, but it seemed that had been it. "What are the two of you doing in this part of the world in the darkest part of the year?" he asked.

"Good question," Zac muttered, still looking a bit shell-shocked from the whole bizarre exchange.

"We wanted to spend Christmas here. I have many happy memories of summers at Eilidh's cottage."

"Aye, but it's winter."

True enough. "I need to get the rest of the things out of my car," Laurel said a bit pointedly. Surely, now that he'd checked them out, Archie could go back to wandering the wilderness, or whatever else it was he did? He looked like a cross between a hobo and Bear Grylls.

"I'll give you a hand," he said, not making it a suggestion she could politely refuse. "And I'll show you around the place—there are a few wee tricky bits."

"Tricky bits?" Laurel repeated. "What do you mean?"

"The Rayburn's got a bit of a temper," Archie answered

with a shrug. "And the taps on the bath upstairs don't always behave." Laurel was reminded of the animated house of the Beast in the Disney film, imagining an angry cooker and a dancing sink.

"What do you mean, exactly..." she began, but Archie was already heading out into the rain, and after a second's uncertain deliberation, Laurel followed him. Zac sloped out after her, and between the three of them they managed to get all the bags and boxes into the cottage in one cumbersome load.

"How long are you staying here for, then?" Archie exclaimed as he hefted a box of tins and packets onto the old, laminate worktop. Laurel hadn't remembered it being quite so grotty, but a spritz of cleaning spray would certainly help matters.

"Just for a couple of weeks, but I wanted to be prepared."

"There is a supermarket on the island," Archie said with a wry look. Laurel couldn't quite make him out. His manner was both brusque and joking, his face craggy and wind-burned, his blue eyes surprisingly bright and deeply creased. Underneath his flat cap his hair looked wavy, unmanageable, and liberally streaked with grey. He seemed both ageless and ancient, the kind of person who was part of the landscape, rooted like a tree.

"Yes, I know," Laurel said, her tone sharpening just a little. She felt defensive all of a sudden. Perhaps it was because of the gun. "I have spent a fair amount of time here, you know."

"Yes, back when you were a bairn." Archie nodded. "I

remember now."

"You *remember?*" Laurel goggled him. Surely she would have remembered a character like him?

"Aye. You and your sister. Bonny lasses, the pair of you, along with your mum, Isla." He glanced at Zac. "This your son?"

"No, my sister's son." An explanation about why Abby wasn't here bottled in her throat, but Archie, thankfully, was not the kind of man to ask nosy questions. He merely nodded a greeting at Zac, who nodded back, seeming more discomfited than Laurel had ever seen him before, but then she was discomfited too, by just about everything right then.

"So, the Rayburn," he said, and started towards the cooker.

Laurel watched him apprehensively as he crouched in front of the old dark green Rayburn and flipped open one of the doors on its front. "This is the control panel," he said as he twiddled a dial. "If I'd known you were coming, I would have turned it on."

If you'd checked your email, Laurel thought silently, and then wondered why this oddball farmer got her back up quite so much. He was just so…eccentric. Which was a trait she normally didn't have a problem with, but she was already feeling touchy and on edge and Archie's confusing manner, brusque, joking, and wielding a gun, was something she did not have the emotional reserves to deal with at present. She needed one thing, one *person*, to be simple.

With another twirl of the dial and the flick of a switch, the Rayburn slowly rumbled to life, like a monstrous beast beneath the cottage's weathered floorboards stirring from a deep slumber.

"There we are," Archie said with satisfaction. "Should be nice and toasty here in a couple of hours."

"Thanks," Laurel said. Until then they could freeze, she supposed.

"Now if it goes out," he continued, "you just need to fiddle with the dial a bit."

"Fiddle?"

"Spin it this way and that. Talk to her nicely." He slapped the side of the Rayburn the way Laurel imagined he might the flank of a cow. "She likes a kind word now and then, but don't we all?" He let out a laugh and Laurel managed a smile.

She couldn't help but wonder if he was making fun of her a bit? Playing up the whole Highland yokel act? But, no, she really didn't think he was.

"If you run into real trouble, you can give me a shout." He straightened, nodding towards the window and the darkened field beyond. "I'm just along that paddock there."

"Sorry, where, exactly?"

"Cut across, towards the sea. The low white farmhouse. You'll find me, sure enough."

"Do you have a mobile?"

He shook his head. "Don't hold with them."

Just like email, then. Archie Campbell was a positive Luddite, which was another thing Laurel normally wouldn't mind. She had only succumbed to a smartphone a couple of years ago, and she wasn't particularly fond of tech gadgets, although admittedly she couldn't live without her laptop.

But, for some reason, Archie's behaviour unsettled her, made her feel prickly. Perhaps it was because of the way they'd met—with him pointing a gun at her. Not the best start to any relationship, not that she would ever be seeing him again.

"All right, then," she said. "Thank you. And what about the taps?"

"I'll show you."

Laurel followed Archie up the narrow stairs, Zac following closely behind her, almost as if he didn't want to be left alone. He probably thought Orkney was full of gun-toting farmers. Perhaps it was.

"So there's a bit of a mix-up with the taps," Archie said cheerfully. "The hot comes out of the cold tap, and the cold out of the hot."

"Right." Laurel didn't remember that from her childhood. In fact, she didn't remember nearly as much as she thought she had—the cottage felt far darker, smaller, and definitely colder than those hazy summer days she recalled with so much sentimental affection.

"But sometimes they switch," Archie continued, and Laurel stared at him.

"Wait, what?"

"Yeah, bit daft, eh?" He smiled, revealing dimples amidst the weathered crags of his face. Laurel wondered how old he was—fifty? Older? It was impossible to tell. "Don't know how it happens, truth be told, but there you are."

"So what do you do when they switch?"

He shrugged. "Wait till they sort themselves out, I suppose."

Thanks for the tip. Laurel bit her tongue. If Archie Mac-Dougall were a character on a show on Netflix about moving to the countryside, the kind of program she normally loved to watch, she'd find him endearingly eccentric. There would probably be an Archie fan club on Twitter, and even women swooning over his decidedly weather-beaten looks. But, right now, Laurel just found him mildly exasperating and definitely strange.

"How long does it usually take," she asked, "to sort themselves out?"

Archie lifted his shoulders in a beats-me shrug. "Who knows? But if you need a bit of a hand, you know where to find me."

Actually, she didn't, since across the paddock could just be about anywhere on the island. Laurel nodded, deciding she'd had enough of his supposedly sage advice. "Thanks very much for everything."

"Not a bother." He turned from the taps, glancing again at Zac, who was loitering in the doorway, hands jammed into the pockets of his ultra-skinny jeans. "How long are you here for, again?"

"Just a couple of weeks."

"Right. Well, that's something. I suppose I ought to be off." He gave them both a fleeting smile that made Laurel feel guilty somehow. Was she being unfriendly? Standing there in the cramped bathroom, hunched because of the sloped ceiling, she realised how tired and hungry she was.

She'd been travelling since what felt like forever, and she hadn't eaten since lunch, a bowl of mediocre soup somewhere near Glasgow. Plus her back throbbed from where she'd scraped it against the window frame. Worst of all, being back at Eilidh's opened an ache inside her she'd tried to forget she had, and that made her feel even more raw, in a way that was taking her entirely by surprise.

"Thank you for everything," she said again. "Especially for not shooting me."

Archie gave her a quick look before his mouth quirked in a small, wry smile. "Aye, that's the spirit," he said, and then he was gone, striding down the stairs and out the front door, a gust of cold air blown in as he shut it behind him.

Laurel made her way to the kitchen, the house feeling empty and smaller somehow, now that it was just her and Zac. She glanced at the heap of boxes in the middle of the room, and wondered if the taps were too temperamental for her to have a bath.

"Right," she said out loud. "Zac, can you get some wood for a fire? I'll put the stew I brought on the cooker..." She hunted for the Tupperware container of stew that she'd made last night, when she'd been imagining a cosy evening tucked up the fire, exchanging jokes and confidences. They'd get there, she told herself. Eventually.

"Wood?" Zac said sullenly. "Where am I supposed to get that?"

"There's a woodpile outside," Laurel told him. "By the side of the cottage." At least there had been thirty years ago.

The Rayburn was emanating a barely-there heat, but

Laurel gamely dumped the stew into a cast iron pot and hoped it wouldn't take forever to warm up. Zac stumped back into the house with a handful of mouldy, damp twigs.

"That's not firewood," Laurel said, trying to sound light and teasing rather than exasperated. She wasn't sure she managed it. "I meant logs. You know, proper—"

"I know what logs are," Zac said, "and there weren't any there."

"There must be—"

"You look, then."

Suppressing a sigh, Laurel headed outside—it was still sleeting rain—to the lean-to on the side of the house where the wood had been kept when she'd been a child. She and Abby had gone out to fetch logs many times, holding their arms out while the other piled logs into them, and then tottering back inside, barely able to see above the firewood in their arms.

The lean-to was still there, no more than a rusted roof of corrugated iron and a few rotted-looking poles to hold it up, but where Laurel had remembered neat stacks of trimmed logs, there was nothing but a few twigs and dead leaves. She groaned out loud.

"Told you," Zac said when she returned inside.

"You were right. I'm sorry." She let out a dispirited sigh. No cosy fire then, at least not tonight. "I suppose, since Eilidh is spending the winter in Spain, she didn't need to bring in firewood for the season." She tried to sound practical but she felt as if she could cry. It would have helped if Eilidh had told her to bring firewood, or better yet, arranged for Archie to deliver some, but why should her aunt have had to do the heavy lifting, when Laurel had made such an unexpected request? She'd be able to buy some tomorrow. It didn't have to be a big deal.

And yet, right then, it felt as if everything was going wrong. The Rayburn had started to clank, and Laurel feared she would soon have to fiddle with the dial, most likely to no avail. There would be no cosy fire, no warming and hearty stew, no bubble bath. The cottage was freezing, and everything was musty and damp and rather awful.

It felt about as far from Christmas as she could possibly be—this was the anti-Christmas holiday, Laurel reflected grimly as she struggled to think what to do. Everything was cold and dark and lonely, a Christmas worthy of Scrooge or worse.

"There must be a space heater somewhere," she finally said. "I remember Eilidh having one..."

"What, like a million years ago?" Zac shook his head, his face a mask of derision, and Laurel couldn't blame him. This wasn't the quaint, picturesque place she'd painted, not by a long mark. Part of her had the mad urge to hop in the car and go home, but that was impossible. There was no ferry until tomorrow and in any case, she certainly didn't have the stamina to drive another nine or ten hours tonight.

Still, the thought was painfully tempting.

"We'll make do as best we can for tonight," she finally decided. "And tomorrow we'll sort out the firewood and the cooker and everything else."

"How?"

"I suppose we'll have to see Archie." She really didn't know what to make of Archie MacDougall. He was like no one else she'd ever met, and she could imagine him laughing at her when she explained how she couldn't start the Rayburn, or find firewood, or basically do anything.

Why'd you come, lass?

Why, indeed.

Laurel squared her shoulders. "I know this isn't what either of us expected, Zac, but it will get better. We'll make sure it does. Together." The last was said hopefully; maybe they could see the funny side, bond over temperamental cookers and lack of firewood...

Zac stared at her for a moment, his lips twisting, his eyes dark and shuttered. "This place *sucks*," he said, and then he turned and walked out of the room.

Chapter Four

S UNLIGHT STREAMED ACROSS the wide oak floorboards of the guest bedroom as Laurel blinked sleep out of her eyes. She'd slept surprisingly well, considering the cottage was freezing, the duvet slightly damp, and the whole place feeling distinctly unwelcoming.

With the sun having finally risen, however, Laurel's mood did, as well. She slid out of bed, grabbing her dressing gown and belting it tightly around her as she took in the view from the window—a tangle of overgrown garden with a weathered wooden gate that led through long grass to a sliver of silvery beach, and then the sea—dazzling blue under a cobalt sky. It was breathtaking, and it reminded Laurel why she'd loved it here so. It was a much-needed reminder.

In daylight, Eilidh's cottage looked even shabbier and yet somehow less strange. Dark, shadowy corners weren't hiding places for spiders or mice, at least not on this morning.

The Rayburn still didn't seem to be working, but the electric kettle was, and the space heater Laurel had dragged out of the dusty loft last night threw off a welcoming if somewhat sterile heat. It wasn't a wood fire, by any means, but it was warm.

Zac was still asleep, and Laurel had no desire to wake him up, grateful to have a few moments' peace at the start of the day—although a glance at the clock made her realise it was already after nine, and the sun had just risen. Goodness.

The kettle clicked off and Laurel made a cup of coffee with the provisions she'd bought, thankful that she'd thought to do a full shop in Thurso before they'd boarded the ferry. Tesco superstore or not, she was glad to have whole milk for her premium ground coffee this morning.

The day looked so bright and welcoming that Laurel decided to open the door and explore the garden, although the still, frosty air made her shiver inside her thick fleecy robe and lambswool-lined slippers.

The garden she remembered from childhood had been orderly, in a wild way—tangles of raspberry bushes and foxgloves higher than her head, masses of lavender that gave off a warm, dusty scent, and a single sunflower poking proudly towards the sky.

Now it was all a mass of dead plants and frost-tipped nettles; Laurel saw a few skeletal-looking raspberry bushes but not much else. It made her sad, wondering if Eilidh was getting too old to take care of her garden the way Laurel remembered her doing, knowing where everything was, letting it spring up naturally even as she tended to the plants with a loving gentleness. She had to be over eighty by now.

Laurel sighed as she sat on the cracked slate step that served as a back stoop, tucking her knees in and balancing her mug on top. If Eilidh were here, would things be better? The cottage would have been warm, at least, and Eilidh would have welcomed them with hot chocolate or soup or maybe even both. Or perhaps the tiffin she used to make, bursting with raisins and marshmallows and chocolate chips.

It all made Laurel feel terribly homesick, like a child longing for her mother. She hadn't had a mother since she was eight, but she'd had Abby, and Laurel missed her now, more than she had let herself in many, many years.

Why had Abby gone off to university and basically never looked back? It was a question Laurel had stopped asking long ago because she was afraid she didn't want to know the answer. Abby had been everything to her after her mother had died—mother, father, sister, friend.

With a dad who didn't know what to do with two young daughters and was always working on shifts, Abby had stepped up and been as good as a mother. Laurel remembered snuggling with her in bed on cold winter mornings. Abby detangling her hair so patiently before school. Making tea—beans on toast with extra cheese, her favourite. They'd eat it together while watching *Blue Peter* on the telly.

But all of that had changed when Abby had gone to uni in Sheffield when Laurel had been thirteen. She'd come back a bit at the start—Christmas, Easter. But by her second year she'd felt like a ghost, always studying, working, or going on cheap student holidays with her friends. Life had become Laurel and her dad—meals eaten in silence, an affection she trusted rather than felt, a loneliness she'd got used to, a hurt she couldn't bear to acknowledge.

But she felt it now, and it made her ache in a way she didn't want to. *Why, Abby? And what on earth is going on with you now? Do I even have the right to ask? To know?*

Laurel sighed. Perhaps when Abby came out of rehab they'd be able to reconnect again, even if she couldn't imagine it now. Or perhaps she could find something different, with Zac. He was her nephew, after all. They ought to have some sort of bond. And in just eight days' time it would be Christmas, Laurel's favourite time of year— a time for family, for forgiveness, for fresh starts. Why shouldn't they have all three?

The cottage might not have turned out to be what either of them had expected or wanted, but it was theirs for the next two and a half weeks, and they would have to make their own merry Christmas, starting now. They'd *make* their own silver lining, instead of hunting around for it.

Her bottom was freezing from sitting on the cold slate, and so Laurel headed inside, switching on the kettle to make another mug of coffee before she braved the shower, woke Zac, and then they headed over to find Archie's farm in the hope that he could somehow put their little world to rights.

Of course, nothing about that optimistic plan went smoothly. The shower was ice-cold, making Laurel whimper as she washed one body part at a time, unable to bear any more than that.

Then she tried to wake Zac, who saw no reason to get up since there was nothing to do.

"We'll go for a walk," Laurel said bracingly. "We need to find Archie's farm, and I'm hopeless at directions. I need your help, Zac."

Her only response was a grunt, but when Laurel went

downstairs to make toast, she was gratified to hear a few thumps from upstairs, and a few minutes later Zac emerged from the narrow stairs into the kitchen, looking grumpy but at least there.

Laurel presented him with two slices of toast thickly slathered with chocolate spread, as she knew he liked it. He muttered something, which might actually have been thank you, and Laurel's heart lifted.

"Did you see the view from your bedroom window?" she asked as she sat across him at the little table, their knees nearly touching underneath. He grunted, and she continued determinedly, "The sea is amazing. When I was little, I stayed in that room with your mum. We both loved it here."

Zac glanced up from beneath his shaggy fringe, his expression suspicious. "She never mentioned this dump to me."

She was *not* going to be stung by that remark. "Yes, well, it was a long time ago. We stopped going when I was eight—your mum would have been fourteen."

"Why did you stop?"

"Why?" Laurel stalled for time, because she didn't know how to answer. She didn't *know* the answer, and she decided honesty was best. "I'm not really sure, to tell you the truth. Eilidh—who owns the cottage—is my mother's aunt—her mother's younger sister. When my mum died, my father didn't take us anymore. It was never an option." Not even discussed, as far as she could remember, but of course she'd been so young. She must have wondered or asked about it, but she couldn't remember now. "My mum—your grandmother—was from here, you know. Her parents ran a B&B in Kirkwall."

"What happened to them?" Zac sounded surly, but at least he'd asked.

"They died when my mum was a teenager, a car accident. I never knew them. Eilidh took her in, and acted as a mother to her, even though she was only twenty herself." Which had made her relationship with Eilidh all the more special. It made her sad to think she'd let it slide these last years.

"I'm not surprised your dad didn't take you back here." Zac pushed away from the table, his plate littered with chocolaty crusts. "Who would *want* to come to this place?"

"Well, I did, for one, and so did your mum. We loved it here." Of that she was sure. Her memories might have become a bit sentimental, but she knew she wasn't making that part up. "But if you're finished, why don't you take your plate to the sink, and then get your coat and boots. We can head over to Archie's farm."

Zac looked as if he wanted to protest, and Laurel braced herself for a sneer or silence—either was possible—but then, to her surprise, he simply took the plate to the sink and then stomped off to the hall to fetch his coat and boots.

Five minutes later they were outside, breathing in the fresh, salty air, the only sound the crying of the circling gulls and the distant, mournful bleat of sheep. Gently rolling hills of tufty grass stretched in every direction, the sea a twinkle in the distance, the terraced hills of Stromness visible far along the road. It was beautiful, in a bleak and remote way, and

Laurel loved it. She breathed in deeply, reminded of how coming back here had once felt like coming home. *And it could again.*

"Right." She looked around, wondering what Archie had meant by paddock—everything was grassy fields. She saw a few sheep in the distance, and decided to walk towards them. Presumably they were his. "I think we should go this way."

She turned right from the cottage, away from the road, cutting through a muddy field towards another one dotted with distant sheep.

"Where are we going, exactly?" Zac asked in a bored voice, and Laurel nodded towards the sheep.

"To Archie's farm," she said with more confidence than she felt. She had no idea if they were going in the right direction. Presumably there were a lot more sheep on the island than just Archie's.

They walked in silence for several minutes, their boots squelching in the half-frozen mud, the deep, startlingly blue sky giving way to thick, billowing clouds. The wind coming off the sea was absolutely frigid, going right through Laurel's respectable three-season parka that had served her well for a dozen winters in York. She dug her hands deeper into its pockets and hunched her shoulders against the wind.

"Where is this place?" Zac demanded after they'd been walking for the better part of a quarter an hour and no homey farmhouse, or building of any description, had come into view.

"He said across the paddock…" Assuming they'd been walking across the right paddock and Laurel had no idea if they had. The whole island was a blooming paddock, covered in tufty grass and sheep. How was she supposed to know which one he meant?

Zac scowled and kept walking, faster now, as if he wanted to lose her behind. With the mud sucking around her boots every time she moved, Laurel struggled to keep up, glancing askance at the sheep who stared back rather balefully.

She was not scared of a stupid sheep, she told herself as she walked even faster. She was just a tiny bit wary. They were bigger than they'd first seemed.

FINALLY, AFTER WHAT felt like an age, a low, rambling, whitewashed building with a slate roof came into view, seeming alarmingly far away, but at least visible.

"I think that's it," Laurel said, panting to keep up with Zac. He had much longer legs, and he was a lot younger than her. He grunted in reply.

Another ten minutes and they were finally there, approaching a muddy courtyard where an even muddier and ancient Land Rover was parked. Smoke curled from a chimney above, the only sign of life, at least until three springer spaniels tore out of nowhere, barking madly as they circled Laurel and Zac, forcing them to huddle together uncertainly.

Laurel wasn't really a dog person. She loved cats, but dogs, like sheep, made her a bit nervous, especially ones that were barking and baring their teeth, looking as if they were sizing her up for a meal.

Zac didn't seem to be much of a dog person either, judging by the way he was suddenly superglued to her side, after trying to lose her for the last twenty minutes.

"Aon, Dha, Tri," Archie called as he strode out of the house, dressed in what looked like the same thing as yesterday. "Heel."

Amazingly, the three dogs obeyed him, dropping back and trotting meekly to his side with no more than a single snap of his fingers.

"They wouldn't have hurt you," he said with a craggy smile. "They were just doing what they always do—rounding you up like sheep."

"Good to know," Laurel said when she'd found her voice.

"Everything all right at Bayview, then?"

"Actually…no. The Rayburn's playing up, and there doesn't seem to be any heat anywhere, and I was wondering about firewood?" Laurel smiled at him hopefully, conscious of how much she was asking. *Fix my life,* basically. *Please.*

"There's nae firewood because Eilidh's in Spain all winter," Archie said. "Did you fiddle with the Rayburn?"

A phrase which made Laurel want to blush or burst out laughing. "I tried."

"Right. Come in, then." He beckoned to them both as he turned back to the farmhouse door. "I was just having my morning brew, and I'm not going to miss that."

Laurel ducked her head under the low stone lintel as she

stepped into the cluttered kitchen of Archie's farmhouse, blinking in the dim light. The place was…a mess.

But it was a cosy, comfortable mess, at least in a way, with laundry drying everywhere, and piles of newspapers stacked in a wicker basket, and plants growing in a tangled riot on a wide windowsill over the sink. Three dog beds jostled for space under a Welsh dresser crammed with bits of china and stacks of post, and the three dogs—Aon, Dha, and Tri—flung themselves into a bed each with doggy groans.

"Fancy a cuppa?" Archie asked, turning to Laurel. He'd stripped off his coat, plus fours, and boots and was dressed in a forest green jumper that looked to be more holes than wool and a pair of baggy, faded jeans.

Without all his crazy farmer kit, Laurel realised he wasn't quite as old and barmy as she'd thought. He had a lean, muscular body, undoubtedly honed by endless hours working on the farm, and a full head of light brown hair streaked with grey at the temples. Closer to fifty, then, she supposed. He raised his eyebrows, waiting for his response, and she realised she was staring.

"Yes, yes," she stammered. "Thank you, that's very kind. Zac?"

Zac was looking around with a kind of baleful curiosity. The cluttered, cosy kitchen was a far cry from Abby's sleek and chic apartment, where chrome, glass, and leather all featured in equal measure, and clutter seemed to be a bad word. In this kitchen, every possible surface was covered— with post, with washing, with dishes.

"Um. Okay," he said, and then, after a pause, "thanks."

Archie took an enormous brown teapot from a shelf above the absolutely massive Aga that took up most of one wall and plonked it down on the centre of the table, sweeping aside a tottering stack of paperwork first. "Cake?" he asked, and startled, Laurel said.

"Er, sorry?"

"I always have a bit of cake with my morning tea." He whisked a domed lid off a delicious-looking lemon drizzle. "Fancy a slice?"

"Oh, er, sure." Gingerly, Laurel sat down at the table. It seemed as if they'd be staying for a while.

Looking at the bakery-perfect cake, Laurel realised Archie might be married. He didn't *seem* married, and he wore no wedding ring, but he also didn't seem like a man who whipped up a Mary Berry-esque cake in his spare time.

Within a few minutes, Archie had cleared more of a space on the big pine table, and they all had cups of strong, sweet tea and large slices of cake.

"Thank you, Archie," Laurel said, grateful and a little bit charmed by his hospitality. "This is very nice."

"Can't starve," Archie answered cheerfully, and took a large bite of his cake.

Laurel followed suit, with a smaller bite. It was delicious—light, lemony, with a sharp tang and then a burst of sweetness.

"This is very good," she said, and he gave a nod of thanks.

"Lemon drizzle's always been my specialty."

"You made it yourself?" Laurel couldn't keep the surprise

from her voice.

"Aye. Didn't think I did, did you?" he added shrewdly. "I like my cakes and biscuits, so it was either learn to bake or go without."

So not married, then, Laurel supposed, not that it mattered. "You've lived on the island your whole life?"

He let out a bark of laughter. "Can't you tell?"

Laurel gave a laugh of acknowledgement. "Yes, I suppose I can."

"Couldn't imagine myself anywhere else," he said. "Never even thought about it."

"No," Laurel agreed. She couldn't imagine him anywhere else, either.

"Your family's from here as well, though," he pointed out through a mouthful of cake. He swallowed and nodded towards Laurel. "Your mum grew up in Kirkwall, as I recall."

"Yes, that's right." Funny how Orkney made her think of Eilidh more than her mum. Her mum was home in Scarborough, humming in the kitchen, snuggling on the sofa, memories so faint Laurel could barely recall them, and when she did, they hurt. So she ended up trying *not* to remember them, which also hurt, in it's own way.

"So you're an Orkney lass, whether you feel like it or not."

Laurel raised her eyebrows. "Even though I've never lived here?"

Archie shrugged. "We remember our own."

Which made Laurel feel as if she were part of something bigger than herself, which was rather a nice thought, even if she wasn't sure she could believe it. She hadn't been back to Orkney in nearly thirty years.

"Right." Archie put down his mug and slapped the table with both hands. "Time to get on, I suppose."

"Already?" Filled with tea and cake, Laurel was feeling rather sleepily content. Archie's kitchen was warm and welcoming, a far cry from the dingy cold of Eilidh's cottage. She didn't feel like moving, much less walking twenty minutes or more through muddy fields.

"Yes, already," he answered with a laugh. "I've got sheep to care for, and a barn to muck out."

"Oh, right." Laurel flushed at her own thoughtlessness. "I'm sorry we're taking up your time…" She wondered if she should offer to pay him for something, but she was a bit scared to. She had a feeling Archie would bristle and refuse, and she didn't want to experience a dressing down in full Scottish brogue. "What's a skellum, by the way?" she asked.

"A skellum?" His slightly shaggy eyebrows rose. "A scoundrel."

"And what's…choring?"

"Stealing. Why are you asking, if I may know?"

"Because you called us that last night," Zac interjected somewhat sourly.

Archie threw back his head and laughed. "So I did. And with my gun pointed at you as well. I gave you the full treatment." He shook his head, still laughing, and, doing her best to see the funny side of it, Laurel managed a small smile. "Right," Archie said again. "We'll take the Rover."

Laurel and Zac pulled on their coats and boots as Archie

did the same, the dogs lifting their heads from the beds before dropping them back on their paws.

Then Archie was marching ahead, half fairy godfather, half taciturn farmer, hopefully ready to fix, well, everything. Laurel exchanged an uncertain look with Zac before they both followed him out into the still-frigid morning.

Chapter Five

OUTSIDE, LAUREL AND Zac followed Archie to the side of the farmhouse, where an impressive amount of wood was neatly stacked under a weather-beaten tarp.

"We'll load up the back of the Rover," Archie said, and Laurel looked at him, startled.

"You mean...all this?"

"You'll need it."

"Oh, but...I didn't..." Laurel stammered uncertainly, before blurting out, "We'll pay you, of course..."

Just as she'd expected, Archie bristled, his shoulders drawing up, his chest thrust out. "Nonsense. I've given Eilidh firewood every winter for twenty years or more. I can do the same for her family."

"Oh...well, thank you." Feeling both awkward and grateful, Laurel held out her arms as Archie began to load her up with wood. And load her up he did, so the stacks of logs went past her head, and she couldn't see anything in front of her.

"Off you go," he said, and she tottered in the general direction of the Rover, hoping she wasn't about to fall flat on her face.

They worked in silent symmetry for a quarter of an hour, loading up with logs and then stacking them in the back of the battered Land Rover. Archie, Laurel realised, could work twice the rate of her or Zac, his movements brisk and efficient, barely breaking a sweat. This was nothing to him, and yet Laurel's arms already ached. At least he didn't make any comments about them being city slickers, although Laurel suspected he was tempted. *She* was tempted.

"Right, hop in," Archie said once the boot was filled to the roof with logs. "And we'll sort out the Rayburn." He slanted Laurel a smiling glance as she climbed into the passenger's seat. "You did talk nicely to her, I hope?"

"Er…I tried?"

"It makes a difference." He almost sounded severe.

"Okay…"

Archie laughed to himself as he started down the bumpy track at a fast clip, causing every bone Laurel had to feel as if it were rattling around in her body. The Rover's shock absorbers, she suspected, were long gone.

Five minutes later, he was parking behind Laurel's car, and then they were doing the reverse of what they'd done before, unloading the firewood and stacking it in the lean-to. It gave Laurel a warm glow of satisfaction to see it there, ready to be used.

"Now for the Rayburn," Archie said, turning inside.

Laurel felt guilty for keeping him away from his proper work, but she was desperate to have heat.

Once inside, Zac disappeared to his bedroom, clearly having had enough socialising for a while, and Laurel stood uncertainly in the kitchen while Archie stripped off his coat and boots and then crouched down in front of the Rayburn as he had last night.

"Ah-hah. Erm. I've got it now…" He continued to mutter to himself as Laurel stood there, feeling like an utter lemon.

When he lay down on his stomach so he could reach into the Rayburn's ancient innards, Laurel edged backwards, strangely transfixed by the sight of his holey jumper riding up, so a thin band of tanned, toned back was revealed. Surely she couldn't be *ogling* Archie MacDougall. How utterly ridiculous.

He continued to tinker and mutter while Laurel decided to make herself useful and unpack some of the boxes and bags she hadn't got to last night. After that, she wiped down the worktops and table, and then dusted the sitting room, plumping the sofa cushions and draping a crocheted blanket over the shabbiest bits, pleased at how the cottage was starting to feel homey.

More and more, Laurel was realising what she'd loved about Eilidh's cottage, and it wasn't the quaintness, the low, beamed ceilings or the cosy fireplace. It was the *memories*, the people who had shared the space with her, the sense of belonging and love, safety and warmth that she'd felt there. And that, she told herself, she could get again, no matter how shabby the place was. No matter how much it hurt to remember how it had all once been.

"I think it's sorted." Archie stood in the doorway of the sitting room, a streak of grease on one cheek, his hair sticking up in a dozen different directions. Laurel hadn't thought it possible, but she feared his jumper had several new holes.

"Thank you so much. I really appreciate all you've done…"

He shrugged her words aside. "Should keep you warm, at any rate."

Laurel came into the kitchen, thankful to hear the comforting rumble of the Rayburn. "That's a lovely sound," she said with a little laugh. "I remember it from when I was little. It used to make me feel safe."

Archie turned to her, his eyes crinkling in a smile. "Eilidh always said how much you and your sister loved it here. She missed it when you'd gone."

"Yes…" Laurel bit her lip. "I don't know why we stopped, to tell you the truth."

Archie frowned. "It was your mother, wasn't it?"

"Yes. I mean, she died." To her surprise, Laurel felt a lump form in her throat. That didn't usually happen. Her mother had been gone so long, Laurel had become quite matter-of-fact about it…or so she'd thought. "I suppose my father wasn't very close to Eilidh," she said. "I never really knew why."

"Jealousy, I'd think," Archie said succinctly, and Laurel blinked in surprise.

"Sorry…"

He shrugged. "Stands to reason. Your mother was an Orkney lass. Your da took her down to Yorkshire or somewhere, as I recall…"

"Scarborough," Laurel said a bit stiffly. Archie's air of

knowledgeability unsettled her. "But what does that matter?"

"Isla always loved and missed it here. That's what Eilidh said, any road. I don't remember her from before. She left when I was a bairn."

"I don't think she missed it, exactly…" Laurel began, but the truth was, she had no idea. Her mother had died when she'd been a child. She hadn't known anything about what she'd wanted, or what hardships she might have faced. She didn't even know what kind of marriage her parents had had, although she knew her dad still missed her. At least, she thought he did. "How do you know all this?" she asked.

He shrugged in something like an apology. "Eilidh's told me bits. And I was around, you know, back then, even if you don't recall." He gave her a crooked smile.

She'd never said she didn't remember him, but she supposed she hadn't had to. "How old were you then?" she asked, hoping the question didn't seem too nosy.

Archie shrugged. "Fifteen, sixteen?"

What? That meant he was only in his mid-forties now…only a little older than Laurel herself. Somehow she hadn't expected *that*, although really, now that he was out of his plus-fours, Archie didn't seem that old. An old soul, perhaps. There was a difference.

"I'm forty-three," he said, as if he'd witnessed her entire thought process. Laurel blushed.

"Right…" A sudden, vague memory was surfacing in her mind like a bubble, from that last summer on Orkney; Abby, being boring, fluffing her hair in the mirror and peering out the window instead of going swimming or into town for ice creams like Laurel had wanted to, all because of some moody-looking boy. Had that been *Archie*?

"Did you have a long fringe back then?" she asked hesitantly. "It kept getting in your eyes?"

"Might have done." Archie shrugged, grinning. "Hard to believe when you look at me now, but I went through a wee bit of a Goth phase one summer."

"Yes, I can't quite imagine it." Archie as a Goth. Goodness gracious. Except, Laurel realised, she *could* imagine it, at least a little, because now she realised she remembered Archie, and she was gobsmacked. "I think my sister had a little bit of a crush on you." As soon as she said it, she wished she hadn't.

A sudden tension seemed to shimmer and twang in the air, an awareness that had *definitely* not been there before. This was a man who wore plus fours and sweet-talked to Rayburns, who had pointed a gun at her and was definitely more than a little bit eccentric, if not downright crazy. Why had Laurel mentioned *crushes*? It made it seem...well, she didn't even know what it made it seem.

"Then she must have been daft," Archie said after a moment. "I remember my hair back then."

Laurel laughed, relieved that the moment—whatever it had been—seemed to have eased. Sort of. "Perhaps I'm remembering it wrong."

"I'm sure you are."

"I didn't realise you knew so much about Eilidh," Laurel said slowly. "And even my mum. But then, I suppose you've been Eilidh's neighbour for a long time."

"My whole life. But I didn't know your mum, not really. Like I said, she left when I was but a bairn. I'm sorry. I didn't mean to upset you by mentioning her. Perhaps I shouldn't have said anything. I don't know aught, not really."

"But you do." Laurel swallowed hard, feeling weirdly vulnerable as she asked, "Do you...do you remember my mum? At all?"

Archie's expression softened as he gazed at her. "A bit, from your visits. She had lovely long hair. And she liked to sing."

"I'd forgotten that." Her mother had sung lilting Scottish ballads as she'd hung up the washing. Laurel could picture her now, in a long skirt and loose top, hair blowing in the wind. "I'd completely forgotten that," Laurel said again, and then, to her dismay, she felt tears crowding her eyes, too many to blink back. Archie was going to think she was an absolute nutter, falling to pieces over so little. "Sorry," she muttered as she wiped her eyes. "Sorry." She let out a choked, horrified laugh.

Archie wasn't saying anything, probably because he was even more horrified than she was. How could she be *crying*?

Somehow, with what felt like superhuman effort, she managed to get her unruly emotions back under control. Mostly.

"Sorry," she said for a third time as she hitched in a ragged breath. "Coming back here...it's brought up all sorts of memories and feelings I didn't expect."

"Bound to," Archie said with a nod and a creased smile

of sympathy. "Since you hadn't come here since you were a lass. Bound to bring some things back up." He seemed reassuringly unfazed by her near-meltdown, taking it in his stride along with everything else.

"Yes, it's just…" Laurel could still feel a lump in her throat, although it was thankfully starting to dissolve. "I came here hoping for some sort of miracle," she confessed with a wobbly laugh. "Isn't that stupid?"

Archie's eyes looked impossibly blue as they creased in concern. "I wouldna call it stupid," he said after a moment. "After all, Christmas is the time for miracles, isn't it?"

"Yes, I suppose. And I have a tendency to…" *Be naively delusional.* No, she wasn't going to admit that. Laurel decided it was time to rein the conversation back in. "Anyway, it's a miracle to me that you got the Rayburn working at long last." The cooker was still rumbling away, and Laurel could actually feel a warm, comforting heat emanating from it, a miracle indeed. "Thank you."

Archie took the not-so-subtle cue and reached for his coat. "Anytime. Let me know if you need anything else."

Feeling a bit as if she'd brushed him off, Laurel said, "Actually, I was hoping to get a Christmas tree today. Is there a place in Stromness where they sell them?"

Archie shook his head. "Not in Stromness, no, but you could get one in Kirkwall, if you wanted, at the garden centre on the outskirts of town. It's about a twenty-minute drive."

"I think I can manage that. Thank you."

He nodded, and then turned to go. For a second, Laurel

had the bizarre urge to ask him to stay, although she couldn't even say why. Perhaps because, beneath his bluff exterior, he really did seem like a kind, old soul, and she could use one of those in her life right about now.

But he had to work to do, and she didn't actually know him from Adam, and anyway she was here to bond with her nephew, not an eccentric sheep farmer she'd most likely never see again. Although she'd thought that once already, and yet here she was.

"Thanks again, Archie," she called as he headed out of the cottage. "See you...sometime."

He waved in response, and then he was gone, the door shutting behind him with a final-sounding click.

Laurel turned to the kitchen, which was looking cosier now that she'd cleaned it and there was a hopefully reliable source of heat. Her sagging spirits started to lift, just a little, although she still had to fight a wave of loneliness from crashing over her.

Now that the cottage was looking homier, she was reminded all the more of Eilidh. She could picture her standing at the stove, or sitting by the fire, always with a ready smile, a welcoming hug.

Standing there, Laurel found herself picturing her mum as well, curled up in the other armchair by the fire, laughing at something Eilidh had said. It was far easier to picture Eilidh than her mum, because she'd seen her, albeit intermittently, over the years.

Her mum felt like a ghost, hazy and unreal. She couldn't remember what her voice sounded like, or the exact shade of her brown hair, or how she'd smiled.

And yet Archie had made her remember. *She had lovely long hair and she liked to sing.*

Yes, she'd had long hair, even if Laurel couldn't remember the exact shade. Long enough for her to be able to sit on it. Sometimes Laurel had brushed it at night, long, sure strokes while her mother had closed her eyes and smiled. She'd had hazel eyes, too, the same as Laurel's—and Abby's. And the same slight space between her front teeth that hadn't been worth the aggro of braces. Actually, Laurel realised with an unsettling jolt, her mother looked a lot like her. Or rather, she looked like her mum.

She was almost near tears again, Laurel realised with alarm. She wasn't normally so emotional, not about her mum, at least. Give her a good rom com or a soppy advert on TV, and she'd be in extravagant floods of tears, but when it came to anything that actually *mattered...*

She drew a quick breath, willing all that emotion back, and decided to find Zac and ask him what he'd like for lunch. Perhaps afterwards they could venture into Kirkwall, to find a Christmas tree.

Zac was lying on his bed in the little third bedroom Laurel had once shared with Abby, squinting at his phone, fingers flying.

"What!" Laurel stared at him in dismay. "I thought you didn't have signal."

"I don't," he said in his usual bored voice. "I'm playing a game that doesn't need Wi-Fi."

"Oh, for heaven's sake." Deflated, Laurel tried to bolster

her spirits set to sag once more. "Well, what would you like for lunch? There's leftover stew or I could make ham and cheese toasties." Zac just shrugged, and Laurel bit her lip, fighting a wave of frustration. If he could just *look* at her... "Please, Zac. I am actually trying, you know?"

Finally, he lifted his gaze from his phone. That was something at least. "Trust me, I *know*."

Ouch. Did he think she was pathetic, pushing for some kind of relationship when he so obviously didn't want one? The thought made her squirm, and resolutely she put it to the side. *Not helpful*. "I thought after lunch we could go get a Christmas tree."

He shrugged. "Whatever."

She had to stop expecting him to morph into some sweet little cherub, Laurel told herself. He was *fourteen*. Maybe most fourteen-year-old boys were like this. They probably were, judging from the few she'd seen loitering about on the streets, looking either menacing or obnoxious, in dark hoodies and low-slung trackie bottoms, smelling of far too much cheap aftershave, hair long and gelled on top and buzzed short on the sides.

Thugs in the making, one of her friends, determinedly childless, had said when a group of boys blocking the entrance to the Shambles in York had refused to move out of the way to let them through. They'd had to shoulder their way through, and Laurel had felt a little frisson of fear at the lads' surly expressions, the simmering testosterone, their unwillingness to move.

Really, compared to that lot, Zac was a saint. Sort of.

sounded indifferent, but Laurel couldn't help but be appalled. She lived alone, and *she* still had a tree, and presents—one for Mistral, at least, and one for her neighbour Helen—and a roast dinner for the friends who were kicking around with nowhere to go for Christmas.

She decorated her little cottage to the hilt, and watched the Queen's speech and all the rubbish telly, and sang Christmas carols at the top of her voice while whipping the cream for her Christmas pavlova and sneaking a tipple or two.

She'd done it all since Abby had done it for her, back when they were little. After Abby had left, she and her father had eaten a roast dinner for two, pulling a cracker and wearing paper crowns… but when Laurel had left home, her father hadn't continued the traditions or seemed to want to, and so she'd only spent a handful of Christmases with him over the years, finding it rather grim to sit in front of the telly all day, her dad only rousing himself to eat the dinner she'd made.

It made her sad to think Zac didn't have any traditions save for a rubbish takeaway. Why hadn't Abby ever seen the point? Because she certainly had when they'd been younger; Laurel had distinct memories of Abby lugging a tree into the house when their dad had been working overtime. She'd put Christmas carols on the CD player while they'd decorated the tree and made popcorn to string with cranberries. She'd even made a roast dinner, because it had always been Laurel's proud job to mash the potatoes. When—and why—had that stopped?

"I don't understand," she said slowly, and Zac gave her a blank look. "Your mum used to love Christmas."

He shrugged. "She never did with me."

"Well we're not having takeaway this year. And we're *definitely* having a tree." Laurel plunged her hand into the basket of baubles and put several into her shopping trolley. "And pavlova, and Christmas carols, and presents and stockings."

Zac didn't reply—no grunt, no shrug, no blown-breath "whatever", and Laurel decided to count it all as a win. She was on a mission. She was going to make this Zac's best Christmas ever, the first real one he'd ever had.

Before too long, her basket was full of ornaments—bright, shiny baubles, cotton wool-bearded Santas, a wooden reindeer, a tiny pair of skis. She couldn't resist any of them, even if Zac didn't seem particularly enthused. *He would be.*

When it was all on the tree, when the Christmas carols were playing, when she'd made hot chocolate and they'd hung up their stockings…

"Stockings!" she exclaimed. "We don't have stockings." Zac just looked at her. "You know, to hang up."

"We never did stockings."

"Not even stockings?" After their mother had died, Abby had always filled her stocking for her. Laurel would wake up to find it at the end of her bed, lovingly lumpy with packets of sweets and small toys. What had happened, to make her sister go from that to this? No stocking, no *Christmas*, for her own child?

"Let's go pick some out," she told Zac, but he shrugged

and turned away.

"I'm going to the café. They have free Wi-Fi here."

Of course they did. "Fine, I'll come find you when I'm finished." Laurel watched him walk off, determined more than ever to make this Christmas count.

She found the stockings in another aisle and picked out two in red felt with white trim. Of course, if they were going to do stockings, she would have to fill them. What on earth might Zac want for Christmas?

She was just mulling this over when her phone rang, surprising her, because she hadn't had signal since they'd arrived on Orkney. Then she saw it was a FaceTime call, coming through on the garden centre's Wi-Fi.

"Soha?" She swiped for the call, surprised and pleased to hear from one of her closest friends back in York, as well as see her smiling face. She'd met Soha on a copyediting course ten years ago, and they'd been firm friends ever since. Soha was no-nonsense to Laurel's dreaminess, cynical to her determined optimism. Somehow it worked.

"I thought I'd ring to see how you were coping. How's your sister?"

"I have no actual idea." Laurel grimaced as she looked around for a quiet place to have a chat without disturbing other customers. She ended up in an aisle with birdhouses and sacks of birdseed that was utterly empty.

"You don't? Why not?"

"The rehab centre is very private, and they've said Abby can't be disturbed."

"I suppose I can see that. How's London then? How's

your nephew?"

"I'm not actually in London," Laurel answered, and then explained about her trip to Orkney.

"Orkney? Isn't that, like, the edge of the world?"

"Pretty much."

"Why did you decide to go there?" Soha sounded horrified. She was originally from Birmingham and thought York was as far north as anyone would ever want to go.

"I've always loved it here, and I wanted to be somewhere without distractions. Zac's constantly on his phone... I feel like I can never get to know him. And I just wanted to get away from, well, everything, for a bit."

"And is it working?"

"Not really." Laurel sighed. "He's so angry, and I don't blame him. The situation is just so awkward and difficult. And he's fourteen, which doesn't seem to be the best age for anything."

"Fourteen was horrible," Soha said with a shudder. "Spots and hormones and everyone is so *mean*."

"Yes." Laurel tried to remember being fourteen.

Abby had left by then, off to uni, and it had just been her and her dad. Loads of takeaways in front of the telly, occasional games of Pinochle by the gas fire, empty evenings alone while her father worked. Tom West had never been a talkative or touchy-feeling man, but he'd been affectionate in his own way.

Why didn't he fill your Christmas stocking, then?

The thought fell into Laurel's head as if from the sky. She was amazed to realise she'd never thought to really wonder about that before. She'd accepted that her father just wasn't like that. When she'd been little, Abby had done everything—Christmas, cooking, cleaning, the lot. That had just been the way it was, and Laurel had accepted it because it had started when she'd only been eight, and she'd liked Abby taking care of her.

But Abby had only been fourteen, the same age as Zac, yet Abby had been acting like her mother, sister, and best friend all wrapped up into one. Making sure she had a bath at night. Helping her with her homework. Plaiting her hair.

Of course, Laurel had appreciated it... *later*. At the time she'd simply expected it, because she'd been small and Abby had been there. And yet...

And yet what?

"Laurel?" Soha's voice broke into her thoughts. "How long are you there for?"

"Sorry...I was miles away for a minute. We'll stay through Christmas. After that, I don't know." She sighed as the realisations of her current problems tumbled through her yet again. "Zac's been excluded from school, so..."

"What!"

"It's a long story."

"It sounds pretty awful," Soha said in sympathy. "You're amazing, for taking it all on."

"I'm not, really. My sister did the same for me, and much more, when we were young." And she'd never really had the chance to say thank you, after all these years. When Abby had left for university in Sheffield, Laurel had only been beginning to realise how much her sister had done for her, and by then Abby had already started to cut those family ties, staying away for holidays, working in Sheffield for the summer. Keeping her distance, which had hurt, and made Laurel not even want to say thank you any longer…so she hadn't.

And as the years had passed and Abby had stayed distant, saying thank you had been just about the last thing Laurel had wanted to say to her sister. *Why?* Might have been top of the list, or *what happened?* Or even *don't you love me anymore?* If she'd been feeling honest and vulnerable. But in truth she'd never really said anything at all.

Now she wondered if Abby had resented her, for having to be taken care of for so long. Or had she resented their father, for not doing it?

Why *hadn't* he filled her Christmas stocking, or bought her a birthday present, or made dinner once in a while? Of course, Laurel knew why. Her father had never done those things. He was a blokey bloke, a police officer who was the son of a police officer, and he hadn't done those things when her mother was alive—or dead. He wouldn't even *consider* doing them. So Abby had.

"Still, it's a bit much to just drop you in it, isn't it?" Soha said with a snort. "I mean, after all these years…"

"Actually," Laurel said quietly. "I don't think it is."

After she'd finished the call with Soha, assuring her she'd be back in York in the new year, Laurel went through the rest of the shop, chucking things into the trolley with determined abandon. Mince pies, fairy lights, a CD of Christmas carols which, they could play if she could find

Eilidh's old CD player, and a few stocking stuffers she hoped Zac might enjoy—a table tennis set he could use on a kitchen table, a harmonica, a Rubik's cube.

She winced a bit at the bill, but told herself it was worth it. When it was all in bags she lugged them over to the café where Zac was sprawled on a chair, thumbs flying.

"What are you doing?" Laurel asked with as much cheer as she could. "What's the latest app for teens these days?" Zac gave her a scathingly incredulous look, and she could hardly blame him. She sounded as if she were about eighty. Why didn't she just call him a whippersnapper while she was at it? "Snapchat?" she guessed "YouTube?"

"Why do you care?"

"I'm just trying to make conversation, Zac. I'd like to get to know you." She decided to try a different tack. "What's your favourite subject at school?"

"I'm not in school anymore, am I?"

He really liked to make this hard work. "When you were in school, then."

Zac shrugged. "Maths."

"Maths, really?" She grabbed onto it with obvious desperation. "That's cool." Zac raised a single, sceptical eyebrow. "I was more of an English lit girl myself."

"Cool," Zac said in a tone that indicated the opposite. Clearly this wasn't going anywhere.

"Shall we go pick out a Christmas tree?" Laurel said finally, admitting defeat.

"Fine." Zac slid his phone into his pocket as he rose from the table. Laurel put her shopping back in the car before they headed over to the outside area where a few dozen Christmas trees were set up.

"What do you think?" Laurel asked as they walked along, inspecting the various options. "Nothing too big obviously, but I can't stand small trees. You've got to *mean* it, you know?"

"I guess."

She pointed to a lanky tree at the end of a row. "What about that one?"

Zac eyed it for a few seconds. "It's got a wonk branch in the middle."

"So it does." One of the tree's branches had a funny kink in it, making it look a bit as if it had a broken arm. Somehow it made Laurel like it more. "I don't want a perfect tree," she explained to Zac. "One that's got attitude. I can't stand arrogant trees." Belatedly she realised she sounded like Archie, talking about tempestuous taps and ornery cookers. But trees were different, surely? They were alive, at least.

"Yeah, I get you," Zac said, surprising her. "If we don't pick that tree, no one will."

"Exactly." Laurel beamed at him, heartened by this small bit of understanding. "Someone's got to love that tree, right? It might as well be us."

"Yeah." Zac nodded. "But it does have a *seriously* wonk branch."

"That only makes me love it more," Laurel said staunchly, and Zac rolled his eyes, but with more humour than she'd ever seen before.

An hour later they were back at Bayview Cottage, struggling mightily to put the tree up in a corner of the sitting room. Unfortunately Laurel had not had the foresight to buy a stand, so she'd rigged up a wash basin from the kitchen and some bungee cords from the car, but it meant the tree was both precarious and lopsided.

"Do you think it will fall over?" she asked Zac as she stood back to inspect their dubious handiwork.

"Yes," he answered. "Really, it's just a matter of when."

"*Zac.*" She rolled her eyes at him, and he gave her the barest flicker of a smile, which made her feel ridiculously happy. Finally, *finally*, her nephew was starting to thaw. Here was the miracle, fledgling as it was. All it had taken was a shabby cottage on the edge of nowhere, a bunch of cheap baubles, and a crooked tree. "Shall we decorate it?"

He shrugged his assent, and Laurel put on the CD of Christmas carols she'd bought at the shop. Both of them jumped at the sound that came out of Eilidh's dusty old CD player.

"What *is* this?" Zac exclaimed as he made a face.

Laurel examined the cover of the CD. "Oh dear," she murmured. "I didn't realise this was a CD of Christmas carols played on the bagpipes."

They listened to an ear-splittingly nasal rendition of *Hark the Herald Angels Sing* as Laurel got out the Christmas decorations. She'd built a fire and Zac had set it alight—a far better use of his pyrotechnic skills than setting a chemistry lab to flames—and now a cheerful blaze was burning merrily.

It was all a bit different—the crooked tree, the screech of bagpipes—but that was okay. They were making their own traditions. They were starting something new.

Once the tree was decorated, Laurel went into the kitchen to start making dinner. Shepherd's pie and brownies for dessert—perhaps she'd make Archie a batch, as well, to thank him, for well, everything. It was the least she could do, and Laurel realised she almost wanted to see him again, and his warm, comforting kitchen.

She started humming to herself, bustling around the kitchen, feeling more optimistic than she had in a long while. This was what she'd been dreaming of and hoping for. Here was the magic.

With the shepherd's pie bubbling away in the Rayburn and the smell of brownies wafting through the air, she went in search of Zac.

He was upstairs, back on his wretched phone. That hadn't lasted very long, but never mind. "Come downstairs," she entreated in what she hoped was a cheerful tone. "Dinner's almost ready and I thought we could play Ludo." She'd found the old board game in the back of a cupboard, and had been thrilled to see it still had all—or at least most—of its pieces.

"Ludo?" Zac didn't even look up from his phone. "What even is that?"

"It's a bit like Parcheesi, or Sorry," she said. "You race around the board, and if the other player lands on you, you're sent back home." He looked nonplussed and she tried for a more cheerful tone. "Come on, Zac, it's fun. And you can't play that game on your phone forever."

"Fine." He tossed the phone aside as he unfolded himself

from the bed, all lanky limbs and longish hair. Laurel beamed at him as she turned to head back downstairs.

"I'll go set it up."

She felt as if she'd staged a scene as she stood in the doorway of the sitting room and admired her handiwork—the fire burning, the lights twinkling on the Christmas tree, the game of Ludo set up on the coffee table, the smell of brownies wafting through the air. Perfect.

Zac came into the room, halting as he took it all in. "I'll just get the hot chocolate," Laurel said happily. They couldn't play Ludo without hot cocoa. She brought the mugs in, topped lavishly with squirty cream, feeling happier and more hopeful than she had since taking the train from York to London nearly two weeks ago.

Zac was standing in the middle of the room as she came in with their mugs. "Ready to play?" she asked cheerfully. She set the mugs down next to the game board.

Zac took another long look around, his hands jammed into the pocket of his super skinny jeans, his face closed. For a second Laurel faltered.

"Zac…"

"Actually, I've changed my mind," he said, and then he turned around and walked back upstairs. A few seconds later Laurel heard his door slam shut.

Chapter Seven

"LAUREL!" ARCHIE OPENED the door wider as two dogs struggled to squeeze themselves between him and the doorframe and Laurel tried to smile. "The Rayburn's not playing up again, is it?"

"No, she's fine." Had she just humanised the cooker? So be it. "I just came by to say thank you." She struggled to hold onto her smile as she held out a tray bake. "I made some brownies…"

"That was very kind of you."

"They're not a patch on your lemon drizzle, I'm sure."

"Come in." He stepped aside and the dogs wriggled out, barking joyfully. "Aon! Dha! Tri!" Archie called severely. "Get yourselves back here, ye big galoots."

Laurel smiled at the sound of his brogue. "Do the dogs names mean anything?" she asked as they came trotting back in and Archie closed the door.

"Aye." He smiled sheepishly. "One, two, three in Gaelic. Couldn't be bothered to think of anything else."

"Works for me."

He looked around, noticing she was alone. "Where's the lad?"

"In his room." Laurel felt the lump of hurt and disappointment she'd been swallowing down for the last hour rise up again. "He's had enough of me, I think, and right now I've had enough of him." Which felt petty and mean, but after Zac's rejection of all she'd been trying for, she couldn't help it. Part of her still wanted to burst into tears.

Archie nodded sagely. "Can't be easy for the pair of you. Where's his mum?"

"In rehab." Laurel felt a bit disloyal for admitting that much. "And you're right, it isn't easy. In fact, right now it feels downright impossible." She was *not* going to cry. Archie had already seen her in tears once today.

She wasn't sure what had possessed her to walk across a muddy paddock in near-darkness with a tray bake of brownies; after Zac had slammed his way upstairs, she'd drifted around for a bit, battling a sense of both hurt and despair, and then she'd decided she needed to get out. She needed to see a friendly face, and the only one around was Archie's. So she'd left a note for Zac, not that he'd bother to come downstairs and see it, and here she was.

"Here we are." Archie rootled around in a cupboard and then appeared, brandishing a bottle of what looked like very dark, very old whisky.

"I don't know if I should…" Laurel began, even though part of her was tempted to grab the bottle from him and neck it. "With Zac, you know…"

"A wee dram," Archie answered with a smile. "It's medicinal, especially when taken with a brownie."

"All right, then." Laurel came into the kitchen, taking a

seat at the big square table that dominated the cosy space. Everything was exactly as it had been this morning, at least as far as she could tell—dogs, laundry, piles of post, a lovable mess that enveloped her with its warmth.

Archie poured them both small glasses and then pushed one over to her. Then he cut two large brownies from the tray bake and passed her one, as well. Whisky and chocolate. What more could she possibly ask for?

"Now, tell me what this is all about," he instructed, except he said *aboot* and it made Laurel smile.

"I don't even know where to begin." Or if she should be pouring her heart out—if that was in fact what she about to do—to Archie MacDougall, part stranger, part fairy godfather.

"Start anywhere you like." He sat down across from her and drained his whisky in one. Laurel took a small sip of hers; she hadn't been sure she liked whisky, but actually, it tasted quite nice. Smoky and peaty and, yes, a bit medicinal.

"Well I suppose it begins when a staff person at a rehab facility outside London called me nearly two weeks ago now, and said my sister had checked herself in and I needed to come to London to take care of Zac." Laurel took another sip of whisky, feeling it burn its way down her throat. "But really, it starts long before that—when my mum died, perhaps, or when Abby left…"

"Left?"

"When I was thirteen. She went to university, but it was more than that." That wretched lump was coming back, growing bigger, making her feel as if she were being strangled from the inside. Laurel gazed down into the amber depths of what was left of her drink. Archie just waited, relaxed in his chair. One of the dogs ambled over and placed its head on his knee. From the corner of her eye Laurel watched him stroke it, his long, brown fingers sliding over the silky fur.

She drew a quick, steadying breath. "After my mum died, Abby did just about everything for me. She made the meals, did the housework, made sure I had my PE kit and my schoolbooks, tucked me in at night..."

A sudden memory, sharp in its poignancy, made her catch her breath. Abby carrying a paper mâché model of the Tower of London into school for her; they'd worked together for hours to make it. Laurel had been so proud.

"Anyway, she was really there for me, again and again," Laurel resumed when she trusted herself to speak and sound normal. Sort of. She picked a piece of her brownie off and nibbled it, more to stall for time than because she wanted to eat it. "And then she went to uni when I was turning thirteen, and it was just as if..." She trailed off, unsure if she could put her hurt into words.

After a long moment while Archie waited, stroking the head of one of the dogs, he prompted, "As if?"

"As if she couldn't wait to get away... from me. She hardly ever came back, and when she did, it was like she wasn't really there. She was always out, doing other things, itching to go back, barely aware of me or our dad. And truth be told, she only came back once twice—Christmas and Easter. Then she left for good, although at the time I told myself she'd come back. I told myself that for years." There was the lump, as big as a golf ball, making it hard to swallow or even breathe. "Sorry, you must think me such a nutter," Laurel said with a wobbly laugh. "Descending on you and telling you all this…"

Honestly, what was she *doing*? She didn't even know Archie MacDougall. The first time she'd met him, yesterday, he'd been pointing a gun at her. She was crazy. Clearly completely crazy, and yet desperate to talk about this stuff that had swum up from the depths of her soul—all the hurt and confusion she'd pushed down for far too long, rising to the surface here and now. But even so, to *Archie*…?

Laurel hadn't realised she'd half-lurched from her seat until Archie reached over and stayed her with one hand; his palm was warm and callused on her own.

"I don't think you're mad," he said quietly. "Just under some stress, maybe, considering all that's happened."

The way he said stress—"strayss"—made her smile again and she relaxed back into her seat.

"Your accent is kind of amazing. Eilidh has one too, I know, and so did my mum, so I'm used to it, but I think I've forgotten. Or maybe yours is a wee bit stronger."

Archie smiled wryly. "Perhaps it is, at that. I couldna change my voice if I tried. Anyway." He poured her another generous slosh of whisky even though Laurel knew she didn't need it. Her head was already starting to spin. She took a big bite of brownie to counteract the alcohol, and Archie followed suit.

"Delicious," he said as he wiped crumbs from his mouth. "Much better than my lemon drizzle."

"No…"

"You'll have to give me the recipe."

She almost laughed at that; she simply couldn't picture this man's man, with his craggy face and crinkly eyes, exchanging recipes like some 1950s housewife.

"So," Archie said once he'd polished off the brownie. "Why do you think your sister left you the way she did?"

"I don't know." Laurel chewed her own brownie slowly. "I suppose she'd had enough. I mean, looking back, I can see how taking care of an eight-year-old when you're only fourteen must have been pretty tough." And yet, had Abby had to leave so drastically? Cut Laurel out of her life? That still hurt. That, Laurel suspected, would always hurt.

"What about your dad?"

"He was around," Laurel said quickly. "It wasn't like he was a deadbeat, or anything like that. But he was a police officer, and he worked all the time. And he's never been…" She paused. "Cuddly." All of that sounded like paper-thin excuses now. Why hadn't she seen through them before? Why hadn't she expected her father to take at least some responsibility?

"Still," Archie said thoughtfully. "It sounds like he left the hard work of it all to your sister."

"Yes, I think he did. More than I was ever aware of at the time." She shook her head as she let out a sigh. "So I can see how Abby might have got fed up. But even so…" That lump was coming back again. Laurel swallowed it down. "I just wished she hadn't left so dramatically."

Archie raised one shaggy eyebrow. "Was it dramatic?"

"Well, not *dramatic*, I suppose. She didn't storm out one day and say she was never coming back. In some ways, I wonder if that would have been easier. Then I would have *known*." She took another sip of whisky and let it burn through her. "As it was, I kept hoping. For a while, anyway. But when she started not returning my emails or voicemails, well, I realised she really didn't—didn't want to be my sister anymore." Laurel managed a wobbly smile. "We lost touch for ages, years really, and then she let me know when Zac was born. She had him by sperm donation, so there was no father in the picture, and I thought it might be a new start for us. But it wasn't."

"Until now."

"Yes, until this call out of the blue. I don't even know what she's in for—drugs? Alcohol? Depression? Really, no clue." She shook her head slowly. "And as for Zac…"

"He can't have had an easy time."

"I suppose not," Laurel said slowly. "I don't really know. He's been going to a posh school, which he just got excluded from, and he won't say two words to me, but I thought we were getting somewhere tonight… until we weren't." Archie waited for more, and so Laurel told him about her plans—the hot chocolate, the tree, the game of Ludo, and how Zac had turned his back on it all.

"I know I'm being silly to be so hurt by it," she said with a sigh. "I know that. But I am, all the same."

"Hard not to. But he might come around."

"Honestly, I don't know if he will. Maybe it was a mistake to come all the way up here. I had such happy memories of Eilidh's cottage, and Orkney, but I think I was counting on some sort of magic to bring us together, like in a film." She shook her head wryly. "I've always been a bit of a romantic that way, expecting things to work out for the best in the end. But if it hasn't worked out for me, why should it work out for me and Zac?"

"It hasn't worked out for you?" Archie repeated with a frown, his glass raised halfway to his lips.

"I just mean... you know... with a bloke. Romantically." Even in her semi-drunken state Laurel heard how ridiculous she sounded. Why on earth had she brought that up? She hoped Archie didn't think she was fishing for compliments or something awful like that. "I've been waiting for Mr Darcy my whole life," she said, and that was when she realised she might actually be properly drunk.

"Mr Darcy?"

"From *Pride and Prejudice*. BBC version, obviously." She had to stop now. Really, just stop.

"Don't think I've seen it," Archie said with a crinkly-eyed smile. He really did have lovely eyes, very blue.

"Don't think I'm surprised," Laurel quipped back. "Colin Firth... all dark and brooding and mysterious, but with a kind heart, of course. Deep down. Really deep down." Her mouth was not getting the message from her brain to stop talking immediately. "I've always had this dream..." But she couldn't go into her dream of how one day, *finally* one day, she'd meet the man and know, just *know*. How he would, too. How it would all fall into place, because while Laurel was smart enough to know life wasn't a rom com, she still believed in the magic of romance. Of true love. At least she wanted to.

It was a dream she'd held onto, even though she'd had to let go of others… like having a mum and dad at home, and a big sister who came back.

Thankfully, she wasn't drunk enough to admit all that to Archie MacDougall. "Anyway," she said, "it's worth a watch." There. That sounded more normal, she hoped. "But here I am wittering on about Zac and Abby and—"

"Colin Firth."

"Right, and you've been so kind… but what about you? You've lived in Orkney your whole life, you said?" In terms of changing the topic, Laurel could practically hear the conversational tyres screeching. Never mind. Archie took the turn of topic in his easy stride.

"Yes, lived in this farmhouse my whole life. Born up-stairs."

"Really?"

He nodded solemnly. "Likely I'll die there, too, if I'm lucky."

"Do you have any brothers or sisters?"

A pause, and then he nodded slowly. "I had a younger brother, Allen. He died of leukaemia when he was just a wee lad. Only four years old."

"Oh, I'm so sorry," Laurel exclaimed. And here she'd been going on, as if she was the only one with some tragedy in her life. Of course she wasn't. No one was.

"I was eight. Same age as you when you lost your mam. It's not easy."

"No."

"Wasn't easy for my mam, either. She folded up after Allen died—like she just couldn't see the point of anything anymore. She left when I was ten, headed down south somewhere. Didn't keep in touch, a bit like your Abby."

"Oh." Laurel's mouth dropped open. Now she felt really terrible. Archie had spoken so matter-of-factly, but what he'd said was truly devastating, even more so than what she'd gone through. "I'm so sorry, that's awful…"

He shrugged. "It was what it was. My dad and I rubbed along as best as we could… he's in a nursing home now, in Kirkwall. Dementia." He gave a little grimace, and Laurel saw the grief in his eyes even though he still seemed cheerful, in his pragmatic, slightly brusque way.

"Still. Here I am, wittering on about my problems, when you've got ones of your own…"

"It's nae like that. One person's problems don't cancel out another's. Right now, for you, it's hard. Nothing changes that."

"Right." Still, she felt badly. Like a big complainer compared to Archie's cheerful stoicism. She never would have guessed he'd had so many sorrows in his life. "I just want Christmas to be a bit magical," she confessed. "I've always loved it." She glanced around the room, noting the lack of Christmas decorations. Did he even have a *tree?* "What about you? What are you doing for Christmas?"

Archie shrugged. "The usual, I expect. Lunch at the nursing home with my dad."

"Oh." That sounded both lovely and depressing. "Well,"

she said impulsively, perhaps because of the whisky, "if you want to come over to Eilidh's after…" She trailed off, unsure what exactly she was inviting him to. A second Christmas dinner? A carol singalong? "For company," she finished a bit lamely. "Or pudding. Or…" Something.

A smile creased Archie's face. "I might do," he said with a nod. "I just might do."

Laurel smiled, grateful that he had a way of making everything feel easy. Comfortable. Even though he'd nearly shot her upon their first meeting. "Well." She rose from the table, her head spinning from the movement. Two wee drams might have been one and a half too many, at least. "Thank you for the whisky. And for listening. And fixing the Rayburn. And the firewood…" The list seemed to go on and on. Laurel let out a wobbly laugh. "What would I do without you?" she said, meaning for it to be a joke, except it sounded far too serious. And she was holding his gaze like… she didn't even know what.

Look away, she commanded herself. *Look away, before it gets far too awkward.* She didn't. For some reason she couldn't. They stared at each other, Archie with his kindly smile, Laurel looking possibly crazed or at least far too intent.

"Good thing you don't have to find out," Archie finally said, breaking the expectant silence. He cleared his throat. "I'd offer to drive you home, but what with the whisky…"

"No, I'll be fine," Laurel said quickly, although in fact she could semi-see herself ending up in a ditch. "Don't worry, please. You've done so much. Really, you have." She was officially babbling. "Thank you," she added as she reached for her coat. "Thank you so much."

"Anytime." He helped her on with her coat when she fumbled with the sleeves, and Laurel let out a little nervous laugh as she missed the sleeve not once, twice, but three times. He must know she was halfway to being drunk. A good Scot like him, he could surely hold his liquor. He'd probably had whisky in his baby bottle, or at least on his gums when he was teething. Hadn't she heard about that from somewhere? Eilidh, maybe?

"All right there?" Archie asked, humour in his voice, as she finally, thankfully found the sleeve. Her head was still spinning, and she was feeling, she didn't even know, *strange*.

"Yes, all right. Sorry…" She turned to give him what she hoped was a reassuring smile, and realised she was far too close, her shoulder hitting him in the chest. "*Sorry…*" She pressed one hand flat against his chest to back up, and then realised belatedly that she was practically manhandling him. Time to end this *now*. "I'm going now. Really."

"All right."

"See you… later." Who knew when? With a flutter of her fingers she opened the back door and hurried, half-stumbling into the night.

The cold air had a thankfully sobering effect, and as she crossed the courtyard she felt the dizzying effects of the whisky trickle away, leaving her clear-headed and cringing. How much of a complete ninny had she made of herself—and *why*?

Archie MacDougall was about as far from Mr Darcy's

brooding inscrutability as it was possible to get, not that she was even comparing them for whatever reason. She wasn't. She couldn't be. She could never, ever think of Archie MacDougall, of all people, with his brogue and his plus fours and his sticky-up hair, like *that*. She was sensible enough to know she wasn't waiting for a real Mr Darcy, but Archie? No. Just, no.

Why not?

Those two treacherous words slipped into her mind and Laurel pushed them away. Not a question she intended to ask, much less answer.

With that firmly decided in her mind—obviously— Laurel strode across the paddock, the sheep's protesting bleats making her jump, shrouded as they were in darkness. They sounded awfully loud, and she wondered how close they were. Did sheep ever attack? Rams had horns, didn't they? Did they use them?

Thankfully she made it through the paddock unscathed, without so much as a twisted ankle or a scraped knee, and came through the back door of Bayview Cottage with a sigh of relief. The sight of the Christmas tree made her smile until she remembered how Zac had walked out on her hoped-for happy evening. Was he still moping upstairs in his bedroom? Could she redeem this evening with him somehow?

She went to check, feeling guilty for having left in the first place, even if he was all of fourteen.

But when she tapped on his bedroom door she received no response, and when she called out and then opened the door a crack, all she got was more silence. Zac wasn't there.

Frowning, Laurel whirled around to check the other two bedrooms, the bathroom, and then back downstairs, even though he couldn't be there.

"Zac?" she shouted, uselessly. "*Zac?*"

Her nephew was gone.

Chapter Eight

LAUREL'S FIRST IMPULSE was to run back to Archie's, and have him solve this as he had everything else. But he couldn't possibly know where Zac was, because she'd just been with him, drinking whisky of all things. How could she have been so unbelievably irresponsible, leaving her nephew alone to go drink alcohol? Even if that hadn't been her original intent.

At least she felt entirely clear-headed now as she threw on her coat and boots and once more headed out into the dark night. She didn't know where even to begin to look, or where Zac might have gone. Stromness was at least a ten-minute walk away, and almost everything in the town closed at five, if not before. Still, she suspected that the dubious delights of the Orkney town, about as far from London's urban charms as one could get, would draw Zac more than stumbling around a sheep paddock, accompanied by a chorus of mournful bleating, which was really about the only other option on the island on a dark winter's night.

Digging her hands deep into her pockets, she started striding along the road to Stromness, panic lapping at her senses and threatening to overwhelm her. What if he did something really stupid? Zac was *fourteen*. It was the age for stupidity. Of course, when Laurel had been fourteen, Abby had already left, and she'd done nothing more rebellious than doing her homework in front of the telly, not that her father had even had a rule about that.

Why hadn't he?

Laurel pushed the question aside, knowing now was not the time to wonder why her dad had been so hands-off during her childhood. As for Abby... when she'd been fourteen, she'd been taking care of Laurel.

Where was Zac?

Laurel had reached the outskirts of Stromness, its main street a narrow lane with cobblestones down the centre, terraced cottages on either side, the harbour glinting darkly in the distance. There wasn't much of anything about; she'd have to walk another ten minutes at least to get to the town's few retail offerings—a Victorian-looking hotel on the waterfront, and a couple of shops that would surely be shuttered by now. Laurel couldn't remember anything else, but she doubted Zac would have ventured this far. Would he? Where *had* he gone?

Stromness wasn't large by any means, but its main street meandered for well over a mile, and Laurel knew she could spend hours stumbling around in the dark, to no good purpose. Surely it was better to go back to the cottage and wait, even if she hated the thought of doing nothing. When, she wondered, did this become an emergency?

Zac wasn't a little kid, after all. He was a teenager, and a Londoner to boot. He could undoubtedly take care of himself. He could almost undoubtedly get into all sorts of trouble. Should she call the police? Did she want to go down that route?

Berating herself yet again for leaving him alone, Laurel turned and walked back through the cold and dark to Bayview Cottage.

Back at the cottage she stoked the fire, as if its cheering warmth would somehow beckon Zac back home, and then ended up pacing the small confines of the downstairs, wondering if she should go back out again, ring the rehab centre in what would most likely be a futile attempt to reach Abby, or go over to Archie's and ask him to help. Caught in the crosshairs of indecision and uncertainty, she did none of them, and instead paced and waited. Prayed.

After twenty endless and agonising minutes, she heard the sound of footsteps outside the cottage, and she flew to the door and wrenched it open, gaping in surprise at the sight of Archie marching Zac up the path, one hand firmly clamped on his shoulder.

"What on earth…" She could not complete the thought.

"You have an escaped prisoner," Archie said cheerfully, one eyebrow raised. "Found him wandering the paddock outside my house."

"What… where *were* you, Zac?" Laurel cried.

"At the Ferry Inn, in town," Archie supplied. "Getting trolleyed, by the looks of it."

"*Trolleyed—*" Laurel repeated blankly, unable to take it in.

"Drunk," Archie explained succinctly.

Laurel gaped. Her fourteen-year-old nephew was *drunk*? Now that she could look at him properly, she saw that it was obvious. His expression was glazed, and he was swaying slightly, despite Archie's firm hold. As Laurel watched helplessly, he hiccupped.

"How was a fourteen-year-old boy served at a pub?" she demanded, even though she supposed that was the least of her concerns right then.

Archie shrugged. "He's a big, braw lad."

"He has *braces*."

"Even so."

"You'd better bring him in." She shook her head, despair crashing over her, making her want to cry. This was so far from what she'd hoped for this holiday. So, so far.

Archie shouldered Zac, who was surprisingly docile, into the cottage. Her nephew half-sat, half-collapsed, onto the sofa, his head lolling back against the cushions.

"I suppose he needs sobering up," she said as she watched him. "I could make him a coffee, but I don't think he drinks it." She looked at Archie, hoping for some advice, because the truth was she had no idea what to do.

"Or you could dunk his head in a bathtub of cold water," Archie suggested with a smile. "The lad needs a firm hand. That's all he's missing."

"A firm hand?" It sounded terribly Victorian.

"Aye. He's had his way too often, as far as I can tell."

"And how can you tell?" Laurel asked, feeling prickly all of a sudden, defensive although she'd only had the care of Zac for a fortnight. "You've barely met either of us."

Archie shrugged. "It's obvious."

Was it? Laurel thought of Zac's history of misdemeanours and his eventual exclusion from school. Had they happened because he'd been given too much freedom and not enough love? What kind of mother was Abby? Laurel had no idea, and all of it—Zac's issues, her ignorance—made her feel so very sad.

"I'm not sure I'm the one to give him a firm hand," she told Archie. Zac's eyes had closed and he sounded as if he were snoring. With a sigh, she went into the kitchen to fill the kettle. "I'm only in charge for another two weeks." Not even that now.

"Two weeks isn't nothing," Archie returned. "Especially in the life of a teenaged boy. It can seem like forever."

"Yes, but…" Laurel frowned uncertainly. "It's not really my place, is it?"

"Your sister gave you charge of the boy, didn't she?"

"Yes…"

"Then it's your place."

Slightly annoyed by his rather highhanded manner, Laurel reached for the tin of teabags and plonked one in a cup. "So what do you suggest I do?" she asked. "What does this firm hand look like? Drag him upstairs by the ear? Shout at him? Take away his phone?"

Archie scratched his chin thoughtfully. "The phone's not a bad idea."

Actually, it wasn't, but Laurel shook her head. "He doesn't get signal here anyway." The kettle clicked off and she poured boiling water into the mug, morosely watching the teabag float to the top. Why, she wondered, did life never turn out the way she kept wanting it to? She'd always been a determined optimist, desperately wanting to believe that the magic was real, and that fantasy could become reality. But it never bloody did, no matter how she tried.

"I don't know what to do," she said, as much to herself as to Archie.

"You could send him to me," Archie said, entirely unexpectedly. Laurel turned to stare at him in confused disbelief.

"Sorry…"

"He could help me around the farm for the day," Archie said easily, as if it were simple, even obvious. "I have a barn that needs mucking out, sheep that need their winter feed, and one or two ewes that might start lambing in a week or two. I'll find something for him to do."

"Oh, but…" She could not picture Zac on a sheep farm. He would be horrified. "He's a city boy, really."

"All the better."

Laurel suppressed a smile at that, even though she still was hesitant. "I don't know."

"It would give you a chance to catch your breath, as well," Archie pointed out. "And you need to do something, otherwise he'll be running rings around you from now till next Sunday, once he knows he got away with this."

"Next Sunday…"

"Just an expression." He grinned, his eyes crinkling into bright blue creases. "What do you think to it?"

What *did* she think to it? A day to herself sounded wonderful, if she were honest, even if that made her feel guilty.

She could do her Christmas shopping, a big food shop, even catch up on her work emails. And maybe Zac did need a firm hand… or something. Whatever she'd been trying clearly wasn't working.

"All right," she agreed. "One day sounds good. We could give it a try, at least."

"Or two or three, if you'd rather."

"I think we'll start with one. But first I should get him up to bed." Laurel glanced at the cup of tea she'd made for Zac, but which she doubted he'd drink, judging from the snores she could hear coming from the next room.

"I'll carry him," Archie offered. "He's away with the fairies now." Before Laurel could reply, Archie had hefted a near-comatose Zac onto his shoulder in a fireman's lift and started up the stairs. Zac startled awake, mumbled something, and then fall back into a stupor. Lovely.

Laurel followed behind them, anxious and uncertain, as Archie laid the boy in his bed, took off his shoes, and pulled a blanket over him.

"You might want a bowl," he advised. "Just in case."

"Oh… right." She went back downstairs and came up with a plastic mixing bowl, which she positioned near Zac's head. Asleep, he looked so young—fair lashes on pale cheeks, a shadow of peach fuzz above his upper lip. She let out a sigh, and then exchanged a wry glance with Archie. He smiled, his expression seeming almost tender, and making Laurel want to… she didn't even know what. Cry? Throw her arms around him? She'd make do with yet another thank you.

After another beat, they both headed downstairs again, Archie making for the front door.

"You've rescued me again," Laurel said with a funny little laugh. "This is starting to become a habit."

"I don't mind." He smiled at her again, and something strange leaped around low in Laurel's belly, making her jolt. She wasn't... she couldn't be... no, of course not. It was just this was a weirdly intimate moment.

"Why don't you bring the lad over after breakfast?" Archie suggested. "And you can collect him at suppertime, if you like."

"Shall I bring something over for supper, then?" she suggested. "As a thank you?" Belatedly she realised how presumptuous she was being, inviting herself over. Archie might have plans for the evening, and yet she realised she wanted to be involved. To see him again.

"If you're not bothered," he said. "That would be grand."

"All right, then." She smiled, and he smiled again, and the moment spun on a second or two too long, before he finally opened the door and headed out into the darkness.

Laurel remained in the hall, her head spinning a little. She'd seen a lot of Archie MacDougall for one day, and she'd see even more of him tomorrow. The thought made her feel... well, she didn't know how she felt, but she was smiling as she turned back to the kitchen.

Chapter Nine

"WHAT? NO. WAY. I am not going." Zac glared at Laurel over the remains of their breakfast, his arms ominously folded, his eyes bloodshot. He'd been sheepish this morning, until she'd told him about Archie's grand plan.

"Yes, you are, Zac," she said as firmly as she could. Now that she'd committed to it, she knew she couldn't back down. "If you think you can scarper off to a pub and get drunk without any consequences, you are mistaken." She met his gaze even though she was positively quaking inside. "Archie needs help on the farm and you're going to do it."

"Archie is *weird*," Zac snapped. "I'm not spending the day with him."

"He is not weird—"

"He pointed a gun at us—"

"There was a reason for that. He's been very kind to us, you know—"

"I could call Childline over this," Zac threatened, and Laurel wondered if he had a point.

Kind as he was, Archie was still a stranger. Was she crazy to be considering this? Committed to it? And yet Archie had known her mum, and Eilidh, and everything he'd done so far had been incredibly kind. All right, yes, he was a wee bit eccentric, perhaps, but so what? Wasn't everyone, to one degree or another?

"You're going," she said flatly. "Get dressed. I'll drive you over in ten minutes."

Somewhat to her amazement, Zac was ready and sulking by the front door when she came down to take him to Archie's farm.

"Thank you," she said, and Zac grunted. Laurel supposed it was better than nothing. Five minutes later, they were pulling into the yard in front of Archie's farmhouse, dogs barking and circling the car before Laurel had turned off the ignition.

"Aon, Dha, Tri!" Archie barked as he strode out of one of the barns. "Heel!"

The dogs fell back, and Laurel gave Archie what she hoped was a sunny smile. "We're here," she said unnecessarily.

Zac slouched out of the car, hands jammed deep into the pockets of his skinny jeans. He wasn't, Laurel realised, dressed in appropriate attire for the occasion, but she could not see him wearing the sort of gear Archie looked as if he'd been born in.

"And I'm verra glad you are," Archie said, his Scottish brogue more pronounced than ever. Laurel wondered if he put in on for Zac's sake. "Come on, lad, we'll get you kitted up."

"Wait—what?"

"You canna muck out a barn in that!" Archie exclaimed

with a laugh. "You'll split your breeks, first off, and those sannies look like they cost a fair bit of dosh."

Zac looked at him in alarmed confusion. "My breeks?"

"Your trousers, lad, your trousers! Come on, I'll see you sorted." Archie clapped a friendly arm around Zac's shoulders as Laurel watched, caught between concern and amusement. What had she let Zac in for? Archie turned back to Laurel with a grin and a wink. "See you efter!"

"Efter...?" Laurel repeated. He was definitely putting it on, at least a little bit. She watched them disappear into the house, the dogs slinking in after, before she climbed back into the Rover and headed for Kirkwall to do some Christmas shopping.

It was lovely to be on her own, but Laurel couldn't quite let herself relax as she wondered how Zac was coping. She hadn't even given Archie her mobile number, not that it would work, but still, it suddenly seemed like a rather foolhardy thing to do, to just drop her nephew off with someone she barely knew.

Except... she did know Archie. She'd confided more in him than she had even in one of her best friends, like Helen or Soha. She hadn't told either of them, or anyone else, just how hurt she'd been by Abby's departure from her life. So why had she told Archie? Why did she trust him so much?

Because, she knew, he was eminently trustworthy, no matter about the small circumstance of pointing a gun at her on their first meeting. He was kind, and he was honourable, and maybe, just maybe, a day with him would turn Zac around... or make her nephew ring Childline. Either, Laurel supposed, was possible.

Twenty minutes later, she'd parked the car and was happily strolling down Kirkwall's pedestrianised Albert Street, a cheerful thoroughfare with an eclectic and interesting mix of independent shops.

Laurel loved nothing more than window shopping or leisurely browsing, and she did both as she meandered in and out of shops, picking up a few more things for Zac's stocking—a pair of socks with sheep on them, some clotted cream fudge. At a jewellery shop showcasing local artists, she found a beautiful Celtic cross necklace wrought in silver, and on impulse she bought it for Abby, hoping she'd have the chance to give her sister the gift.

Then she wondered if she should get something for Archie, considering he was—maybe, sort of—spending Christmas with her and Zac, and also as a thank you for all he'd done. Laurel bought a Mary Berry cookbook specialising in cakes, happy with her purchase, at least until she saw the sky-blue men's jumper in the window of a wool shop. It was gorgeous, and almost the exact colour of Archie's eyes, which was a little disconcerting to realise she knew that. She thought of the jumper he'd worn today that was more holes than not, and decided to buy it, although afterward she wondered if it was too much, too personal.

She'd pass it off as joke, Laurel decided, and say something about how much he needed a jumper. Still, she felt a little nervous about giving him two gifts when he almost certainly wasn't going to give her anything.

With her shopping done, she treated herself to a toasted

sandwich and hot chocolate in a cosy tearoom, enjoying simply sitting and sipping as she people-watched, although after about an hour she felt a surprising twinge of loneliness.

Laurel was used to being on her own. She had been single all her adult life, save for a few casual boyfriends that had sadly never made it past the fourth or fifth date. Her friends said she was too picky; Laurel preferred the word discerning. In any case, she'd usually been the one to end it, simply because she hadn't seen it going anywhere. But it meant that she'd learned to be happy in her own company, and didn't need other people for amusement.

Yet, right then, as she sipped her hot chocolate and watched a family laugh and chatter about their Christmas plans at the table next to her, she felt it again. That twinge, the emotional equivalent of a toothache. She wanted something—*someone*—but she didn't even know who, or what.

Abby? Her dad? A mythical husband as well as a couple of kids? Maybe just her cat Mistral, sitting on her lap and purring as loudly as a car motor. Something. *Someone.*

Laurel sat there for a moment, that empty feeling whistling through her. She'd always wanted to meet Mr Right, of course, but this felt like something else. Something deeper. A need, an ache, and one that wasn't going to go away on its own. She finished her hot chocolate and went to pay at the till, deciding she'd had enough introspective melancholy for one morning. She needed to go to the Tesco Superstore and buy the ingredients for the shepherd's pie she was planning to bring to Archie's that evening.

As she was leaving the café, she noticed a corkboard with

notices pinned on it and spent a few minutes browsing the offerings—a knitting circle, a cinema club, a veg box scheme, a music class for parents and toddlers. Orkney had a lot going on, Laurel mused, before she read a brightly-coloured poster for a ceilidh in the waterfront hotel in Stromness in three days' time, just before Christmas. That would be fun to go to… if she could cajole Zac to such a thing.

SEVERAL HOURS LATER, after a food shop, a much-needed nap, and an hour in the kitchen cooking, Laurel was heading back over to Archie's, the Rover bumping down the rutted track as she eyed the foil-covered casserole dish on the passenger seat. She definitely did not want to spill gravy onto Abby's posh leather seats.

It was only half past five but the sun had long since set as Laurel parked in the farmyard, warm light spilling from the kitchen windows. She felt a mix of apprehension and curiosity as she got out of the car, setting off a chorus of barking from inside the house.

She'd just taken the shepherd's pie from the passenger seat when Archie opened the kitchen door. He was dressed in his usually holey jumper and jeans, his hair sticking up in several directions, a big toe sticking out of a hole in his thick wool socks.

"You're right on time," he called to her as one of the dogs stuck its head out from behind him and started sniffing. "We're just having a brew."

"How was it?" Laurel asked as he stepped aside and she came into the kitchen, which was as bright and warm and messy as ever.

"It was all right," Archie said. "Shall I take that?" He liberated the shepherd's pie from her grasp and put it on top of the Aga. Laurel blinked at the sight of Zac lounging at the kitchen table, cradling a huge mug of tea. Was that her nephew? His hair was sticking up as much as Archie's, all artful traces of gel gone. He wore a waffle-weave shirt in dark green and a pair of jeans that were far from his usual look, which was to make it seem as if his trousers had been affixed to his limbs with super glue.

"Hey," he said, and Laurel blinked at him several times before she found her voice.

"Hey. How was it?"

Zac shrugged. "Okay, I guess."

"He did all right," Archie pronounced, giving Zac a bone-jolting clap on his back. "The lad did all right."

Laurel watched in disbelief as Zac's mouth quirked in a tiny smile. Had he actually *enjoyed* mucking out barns for the day?

"That's great," she murmured, and accepting a mug of tea from Archie, she sat down at the table. "The shepherd's pie just needs warming up," she told him. "We can eat whenever you like."

"Right, I'll pop it in to warm up, then," Archie answered.

It was all very cosy, Laurel thought, as the three of them sat around the table and drank tea while the pie warmed in the oven. One of the dogs, she didn't know which, came and sat down next to her, resting its head on her knee. Another one stood by Zac and he stroked it absently as Archie went through all the work they'd done that day—mucking out barns, feeding sheep, and generally working hard and getting dirty, by the sounds of it.

Although he was quiet, Laurel could tell Zac had enjoyed the day; a satisfaction emanated from him like some sort of glow. As she sat there, listening, Laurel realised she was feeling the *slightest* twinge of jealousy, that Archie's tough love and crazy Scots act had got farther with Zac than her baking, coddling, and Christmas tree had, and she was ashamed of herself for the entirely uncharitable feeling.

What did it matter how it had happened? The important thing was that Zac seemed happy and settled. And, amazingly, in this moment, he did.

Laurel let herself relax as they continued to chat, and then, a short while later, it felt weirdly natural to lay the table while Archie retrieved the shepherd's pie from the Aga, opened a bottle of elderflower cordial—"non-alcoholic" he assured her with a wink—and they sat and eat as they debated about which Marvel superhero film was the best. Laurel hadn't seen any of them, so she let Archie and Zac hash it out; apparently they were both big fans, and she was both touched and the tiniest bit discomfited to see how animated Zac had become as he debated the merits of Thor versus Captain America.

After they'd eaten, Archie asked Zac to check on the animals for the night.

"By myself?" Zac looked slightly alarmed at the notion.

"You can do it, lad. You know how."

Laurel watched him go, shaking her head as Zac pulled on his boots and coat and headed outside. She rose from the table and began clearing plates.

"You seem to have had the knack," she remarked as she went to the sink and began to fill it with water.

"Maybe he just needed something different."

"Yes." Laurel squirted some dish soap into the hot water and swished it around. "It seemed he did."

Archie brought an armful of dirty dishes to the counter. "You wash, I'll dry?"

"All right."

It was comfortingly companionable to wash the dishes in silence, the clink of cutlery and clank of plates the only sound, punctuated by the occasional doggy groan from Aon, Dha, or Tri.

"What is it?" Archie asked after a few minutes and Laurel glanced at him in surprise.

"What do you mean?"

"You've got a bee in your bonnet about something. I can tell."

"I don't..." Laurel began before faltering at Archie's craggy, knowing smile. "I don't, really," she amended.

"What is it?"

It felt too petty to say. She didn't really feel it anyway, at least not *much*.

"Well?" Archie prompted.

"It's just I've been trying so hard," Laurel burst out. "And nothing's worked. Not the brownies, not the Christmas tree, not all the time and effort… and then you swan in and make him muck manure, and somehow *that's* the miracle?" She let out a raggedy laugh. "Sorry, I know I sound like an absolute twit. I do, but—"

"I understand."

"Do you?" Laurel turned to look at him. "I feel ridiculous and selfish for even saying that much—"

"They go together," Archie told her. "You can't have the manure without the brownie."

Laurel let out an uncertain laugh. "That's surely a motto to live by."

"Works for me," Archie answered with a grin. "And don't fret yourself over Zac. He's feeling his way, and to be sure it will take some time. Today wasn't magic, much as you might be looking for it."

Laurel let out an uncertain laugh. "I always seem to be looking for some magic," she admitted on a sigh. "I don't know why."

"Aren't we all, in one way or another?" For a second, Archie looked bleak, and Laurel remembered the sorrows he'd already faced in his life. Why, she wondered, had he never married, had children? Had he wanted to? Was there a woman whom he'd lost, or a relationship that hadn't worked out?

"Yes, I suppose we are." And one day, she hoped, she'd find it. For Zac, for Abby, for herself and the Mr Right she still believed was out there somewhere, wherever she might find him.

"Magic isn't something you can force," Archie said gently. "And the more you try, the less the chance there is of it happening."

"So you think I should just relax and let things happen with Zac?" she surmised.

"Something like that, I suppose."

The door to the kitchen opened, bringing in a gust of cold air. "They're all fed," Zac announced, and Archie filled the kettle and plonked it on top of the Aga.

"Time for a game of Monopoly, then."

"Monopoly?" Zac looked dubious.

"I've never lost at it yet," Archie announced as he retrieved a battered box from a cupboard. "But I bet you can give me a run for my money, lad."

"What about me?" Laurel asked in mock indignation.

Archie winked at her. "You already are."

If she hadn't known better, she would have thought he was flirting. If she hadn't known better, she almost wished he was.

They played an epic game of Monopoly over tea and the last of Laurel's brownies, with Archie winning rather smugly.

"It's the oranges," he explained as they tidied away the pieces. "Always go for the oranges."

"That's your trick?" Laurel said with a laugh. "And you've just given it away?"

"I've got plenty more." He tapped his forehead knowingly before turning to Zac. "Whole theories on railroads, when to build houses, the lot. See you tomorrow?"

"Wait, what?" Laurel looked at them both blankly.

"I could use another day of help," Archie explained easily. "If Zac wants to pitch in. I told him I'd pay him this time. Not much, but a little." He glanced at Laurel. "If that's all right."

What could she say but yes? "If Zac wants to…" She glanced at Zac, who shrugged his assent. He didn't look thrilled, but he didn't look put out, either. Laurel suspected he was simply playing it cool.

"Right, okay, then. I can drop him off…"

"I'll walk," Zac said unexpectedly. "I don't mind."

"All right." Which left her with another day on her own, something that had been lovely today but felt the tiniest bit empty tomorrow. "Great."

"You can come for dinner again, if you like," Archie offered. "But this time I'll cook."

"Oh…"

"Or not," he said with a shrug and a smile. "As you like."

She didn't know what she liked. Laurel tried to sift through her tangle of emotions—hope, surprise, that stupid little dart of jealousy, pleasure. "Okay," she said after a moment. "That sounds lovely. Thank you."

Archie smiled again, and Laurel thought how easy he was to be with. "Thank you," she said again, and then they were heading out into the night, the sky dark and clear, scattered with a thousand stars.

Laurel took a deep breath of cold, crisp air, let it fill her lungs. It was only five days to Christmas now. She wondered how Abby was, if the rehab was working, if somehow this strange stint could bring everybody back together again, stronger than ever before. Above her, the stars glittered and twinkled, like bits of promise.

"Are we going?" Zac asked. Clearly he was not having a moment, the way she was.

"Yes," Laurel said with both a sigh and a smile. "We're going."

Chapter Ten

OVER THE NEXT few days, life fell into a new and surprising pattern, yet one that felt strangely easy in its familiarity and comfort. Zac spent the days working with Archie on the farm, and Laurel joined them for dinner and an evening of playing cards or board games.

The second night, Archie made a delicious beef stew; the following night they all made homemade pizzas. He taught Zac chess, and Laurel satisfyingly thrashed them both at Ludo, although admittedly Zac won the rematch.

She was enjoying these evenings far too much, she thought as she and Zac drove home one night, four days after he'd started helping Archie out. The easy conversation, the fun banter, the feeling of belonging that was so *odd,* because if anything, they were three misfits who had been flung together due to circumstance more than design. But it was going to be hard when it all ended, in just a week, if not before then. It was starting to feel normal, when it was anything but.

Despite the days at the farm and the evenings all spent together, Zac still wasn't talking much to her, although he'd started to relax a little bit, and his phone wasn't as surgically attached to his hand as it had been before.

In the evenings, when Zac went to check on the animals, Laurel and Archie had had chats about island life, farming stuff, and her job as a copyeditor. It had all been very relaxed and casual, but nice. Really nice. Nicer than anything Laurel had done in quite a while.

The day of the ceilidh, Soha Skyped her again, while Laurel had been catching up on work in a coffee shop in Stromness.

"So how are things in the middle of nowhere?" she asked cheerfully. Laurel glanced around the café, grateful there was only one other customer, and he had headphones on.

"More like the edge of nowhere, but they're good. Surprisingly good."

"The nephew isn't as terrible as he first seemed?"

"He was never terrible," Laurel protested, feeling a surge of loyalty for both Abby and Zac. "Misunderstood, maybe. Very misunderstood. He hasn't had an easy time of it."

"Neither have you."

"It hasn't been that bad."

"So what's changed?" Soha asked, and Laurel explained about Archie and how Zac was helping on his farm.

"Seriously? The sexy farmer saves the day?"

Laurel nearly choked on her mouthful of tea. "He's not sexy." That was about the last word she'd associate with Archie, with his sticky-up hair and holey jumpers, his craggy face and creased eyes, although they *were* a lovely shade of blue...

"What is he, then?" Soha asked.

Laurel paused as she recalled the evenings spent in Archie's cosy kitchen, the heart-to-hearts she'd had with him that had felt both weird and natural. "He's kind," she said at last. "He's very kind."

"Well, that's something, I suppose," Soha replied, sounding dubious. "But at least he keeps the nephew out of your hair?"

"Yes, although I miss him a bit, actually." Four days of alone time had been plenty, Laurel was finding. She'd bought all her Christmas presents, caught up on work, and baked more Christmas treats than she or Zac or even Archie could possibly eat.

She'd even had time to visit some of Orkney's sights— the ruins of the prehistoric village, Skara Brae, and the mysterious Standing Stones of Stenness, an ancient circle of tall, thin slabs with angled edges that stood guard over the western part of the island.

"Just one more week, right?" Soha said with a rueful smile. "I miss you."

"I miss you, too." And yet, to her surprise, Laurel realised she wasn't missing her life in York nearly as much as she had been, back in London. The thought of leaving Orkney in just a little over a week—after New Year's—felt like a wrench, which was somewhat ridiculous, she knew, and yet still *was*.

After finishing her chat with Soha, Laurel decided to head back to Bayview Cottage to get ready for the evening. She'd agreed to bring dinner over to Archie's, but she and Zac would be leaving after they ate, for the ceilidh in Stromness.

She hadn't told Archie their plans, and she'd dithered about inviting him along, but something in her had hesitated, and she didn't even know what or why. Was it because she didn't want it to seem like she was asking Archie out or something ridiculous like that, or because she wanted some time alone with Zac? Or something else? Laurel had no idea. Her thoughts were the mental equivalent of a dog chasing its own tail.

As it turned out, the whole issue was a nonstarter, because when she got to the farm and explained that they'd have to leave right after supper, Archie nodded in his easy way.

"I do, as well, so that's fine."

"Oh, okay," Laurel said, slightly disconcerted. "Well, I hope you're doing something fun."

"Oh, aye, taking my dad out." He smiled. "He likes a spin around town now and again."

"That's nice." Laurel felt both strangely disappointed and relieved that she hadn't asked him to come with them to the ceilidh; he hadn't even asked what her plans were. Well, that was fine. He'd never been the nosy type, after all.

Yet she still felt slightly out of sorts as she listened to Archie and Zac debate the merits of different kind of sheep feed—who ever would have thought her nephew would have an interest in such a thing, never mind an actual opinion on it—and then tidied up.

"I suppose we should get going," she said, once the dishes were washed, dried by Archie, and put away.

"Yes, I need to get my skates on, as it is." He checked his battered-looking watch with a grimace.

"I'm sorry if I've made you late—"

"Not at all." He turned to Zac, who was by the back door, putting on his coat. "Happy Christmas, lad. Perhaps you'll do a few days for me in the new year?"

Zac nodded, and with a jolt Laurel realised tomorrow was Christmas Eve. "You'll still come to us on Christmas?" she asked. "After you've been with your dad?"

"Wouldn't miss it," Archie replied cheerfully.

Laurel had the sense that time was slipping away far too fast, and she didn't like it. "All right," she said at last. "See you then."

Zac was quiet in the car on the way back to the cottage, and then Laurel tidied the kitchen while he took a quick shower before they decided to walk into Stromness for the ceilidh.

"What is this thing, anyway?" he asked as they headed down the darkened street towards the town.

"A ceilidh? It's a country dance. Lots of swinging partners round and things like that." Zac made a noncommittal noise, and Laurel was just glad he'd agreed to go. "Are you having a good time here, Zac?" she asked hesitantly. She'd been afraid to ask him so directly before. "Are you glad you came?"

He shrugged, making some sort of mumbling assent, and Laurel decided she would take it as a yes. It was progress, of a sort, and she was coming to realise that what Archie had said might be true—she couldn't force the magic.

As they came into town, she saw the narrow streets were strung with bright, multi-coloured lights, with a huge Christmas tree in the square, people streaming towards the hotel on the waterfront, creating a buzz of anticipation. Even Zac seemed to catch the mood as they joined the crowd—well, crowd by island standards, anyway—and headed for the hotel.

The ceilidh was already in full swing as they came into the hotel, a band with several fiddles, banjos, and other instruments Laurel didn't even recognise belting out a merry tune. The hotel's ballroom was decked out in evergreen and tinsel, with an enormous tree perched in one corner, glittering with lights and shiny baubles. Laurel's heart lifted at the sight of it all.

She headed to the bar for soft drinks, and she and Zac sat sipping their lemonades as they watched a country reel, with partners dosey-doing and flying around.

"Shall we give it a go the next time?" Laurel asked and Zac looked taken aback.

"Seriously?"

"Why not?"

He shrugged. "Okay, I guess."

She smiled, and Zac smiled back. This was going to be fun.

A few minutes later, a new dance was called and they took their places in the circle. Laurel's head spun along with her body as she tried to follow the directions, going this way and that, spinning in a circle, linking arms. She barely knew what she was doing, but she was having fun, and when she glimpsed Zac linking arms with a teenaged girl across the circle, her spirits lifted even more. Maybe, just maybe, it was all going to be okay.

The realisation shuddered through her, as she acknowledged just how tense and stressful she'd found taking charge of her nephew's care. How afraid she'd been, without even realising how much, for Zac's well-being. For Abby's, whose she still didn't know. For everything, and still so much was uncertain, yet right now she had a glimpse that it could, just maybe, be okay, and it was such a relief.

The dance ended, and the circle re-formed, with Laurel smiling and out of breath. Within a few seconds, the music started again, and she started forward to link arms with the person across the circle, only for everything in her to jolt when she realised who it was.

"Archie…"

"In the flesh." He grinned as he linked arms with her. "If I'd known you were coming to the ceilidh…"

"But I thought you were taking your dad out!" Belatedly Laurel was noticing how different Archie looked. He'd combed his hair into some semblance of order, although some still sprang up, and he was wearing a button-down shirt in blue check that was neatly pressed, with a pair of jeans that were not his usual, baggy, mud-splatted work-wear. And he smelled… nice. Some sort of bay rum aftershave, very old-fashioned, and exactly what she might have expected him to wear.

"I am," Archie replied as they reeled around. "He's watching over there." He nodded towards the corner, where

Laurel glimpsed a slightly blank-eyed man in a wheelchair, nodding along to the music. He had the same sticky-up hair as Archie, but it was all white.

"Oh… right." Laurel's emotions felt as if they were tilting and sliding into each other, so she didn't know what she felt anymore. Archie danced back to his side of the circle, and Laurel linked arms with her next partner, a middle-aged woman with a loud laugh who might have had *slightly* too much to drink. She glanced again at Archie, who was dancing with a young woman in a slinky dress. She looked away, focusing on the reel, pushing away all the confusing things she felt, because she didn't know what any of it meant.

Two dances later, Laurel was out of breath and breaking a sweat. She retreated from the dance floor, noting that Zac seemed to have made friends with a couple of kids his age, and they were all goofing off in a corner of the room. She realised she hadn't seen him smile like that before. Properly.

She fetched herself another glass of lemonade and took it to one side of the dance floor, sipping it slowly as she scanned the room, realising only after her gaze trained on Archie bending down to talk to his father that she'd been looking for him.

Laurel took another sip of lemonade, more of a gulp. He really did clean up nicely, she had to admit, in a folksy, farmerish sort of way. She drank more lemonade.

Another dance started, and when Laurel's gaze wandered back to Archie, he caught her eye and smiled. She blushed and smiled back, embarrassed to have been caught staring, and then Archie beckoned her over.

She couldn't exactly ignore his invitation, not that she wanted to, but Laurel still felt uncertain as she crossed the ballroom, wending in and out of clusters of people, until she stopped in front of Archie and his father.

"Hello."

"Laurel, meet my father, William." Archie put a gentle hand on his father's shoulder, his expression turning almost tender. "Dad, this is Laurel. A Sassenach, to be sure, but a friend all the same."

Laurel laughed a little bit at that. "The only place I've ever heard that word is in *Outlander*."

"Where do you think I heard it?" he answered with a wink, and Laurel laughed again.

"Pleased to meet you, lass," William said, "wherever you hail from."

"Thank you. Pleased to meet you, as well."

"Shall I get you a drink, Dad?" Archie said. "A pint of bitter?"

"Aye, that would be fine, lad, thanks."

Archie turned to Laurel. "And you?"

"I'm fine, thanks," she said, hoisting her half-drunk lemonade.

"I'll be back in a tick."

Left alone with William, Laurel cast around for something to say. "Archie has been so kind, taking my nephew under his wing," she said after a moment, and William looked at her blankly.

"Eh?"

"Archie. My nephew. He's helped him…" she trailed off, because the confused look on William's face made her realise this might have been too much to follow. "My nephew has been helping Archie out on the farm," she explained more slowly. "Just for the last few days…"

William shook his head. "Archie?" he repeated. "Who's Archie?"

For a second, Laurel simply stared, her mouth dropping open. Archie had told her his father had dementia, of course, but she hadn't realised it was as bad as that.

"Sorry," she said quietly. "I thought you knew him."

Archie came back a few minutes later, and it only took one quick glance for him to clock what was going on. "Let's get you into the quiet, Dad," he said. "There's a bit of a din in here." He gave Laurel an apologetic look. "Sorry…"

"No, no…"

She watched him wheel William away, her heart aching for them both. She was still standing there when Archie returned a few minutes later.

"He's watching telly with Madge, at reception," he explained. "She's got a bit of a soft spot for him."

"Oh, that's good." Laurel smiled wistfully. "It must be nice, living in such a small, close-knit community."

"It has its pluses, as well as its minuses."

"Which are?"

"You can't sneeze in your own kitchen without Fiona at the post office asking you about your cold." Archie smiled and shrugged. "I don't mind. It's better than the alternative, which is no one knowing you at all."

"True…"

"But you must have some sort of community in York."

"Yes, I suppose…" Laurel thought of her handful of friends, her kindly neighbour. Yes, she did have community, but it wasn't anything like this, not that she even knew what *this* was. Like so much in her life, it felt out of reach, a shimmering promise she longed for but couldn't trust.

The life she'd constructed for herself—her little terraced house, her copyediting work, her cat, her friends—all of it sometimes felt like nothing more than a placeholder, something to pass the time until her real life began. She loved it, she really did, but she'd never thought it would be forever.

But what if it was? What if that was all she'd ever have? What if the magic she'd been waiting for, the hero who was going to sweep her off her feet, never came?

It was a question Laurel had never allowed herself to ask before. It was one she didn't want to answer now. All her life she'd been waiting. What if that was all her life *was*?

Goodness, she was sounding maudlin, she realised with a jolt. And she wasn't even drinking! What was wrong with her? Tomorrow was Christmas Eve, and it had been such a pleasant week…

Yet right then she almost felt near tears, and she wasn't even sure why.

"Laurel?" Archie cupped her elbow with his hand, his touch firm, his palm warm through her jumper. "Are you all right?"

"Yes…" She nodded, a force of habit more than anything else. Of course she was all right. She was always all right. She was a cheerful optimist, always looking on the bright side, always finding that silver lining, or at least searching for it, determined to find it one day...

But what if she didn't?

"Come on," Archie said, and, taking her by the elbow, he led her out of the crowded ballroom, and then out of the hotel, into the cold, dark night, the harbour gleaming blackly in front of them, the waterfront still and silent.

Laurel drew a shaky breath. "Zac..."

"Looked like he found some mates. He'll be fine for a moment."

"I'm fine..." she protested, all too feebly.

"Are you sure about that?" Archie asked quietly and Laurel leaned back against the hotel's brick wall, dragging a deep breath of cold, clear air into her lungs.

"I've always been fine," she said, as much to herself as to Archie. "I'm not going to fall apart now."

"There's no harm in it, you know."

"What?" She turned to him in surprise. "Falling apart?"

"A little wobble, at least," Archie said with one of his grins that creased his face and crinkled his eyes. "You've had a hard time of it lately..."

"It's not that. At least, it's not just that." Laurel drew another shuddering breath. "It's everything. It's remembering the past and thinking about the future..." The words started to spill out of her, tripping over themselves. "Coming back to Orkney... it's made me remember all sorts of things. Being a child. Missing Abby. Missing my mum. Wondering why my dad never stepped up once—" She clamped her lips together, because she was afraid if she said anymore, never mind a little wobble, she'd be in absolute pieces.

"All this stuff I didn't think bothered me anymore. I'd got over it, if I'd ever even needed to. And all that makes me think about the future. What if this is all there is? What if I never find what I'm looking for? What if it doesn't get any better?" She knew Archie couldn't answer those questions, and she hated having to ask them. "Don't mind me, honestly. I'm fine, I really am." She said the last almost fiercely, turning to practically glare at Archie.

"Ah, lass," Archie said with a wry smile, "No one's fine."

His compassionate gaze was like a hand reaching right into her heart. It *hurt*. "Not even you?" Laurel asked, a slight wobble to her voice.

"Definitely not me."

"But you seem so…"

"I make the best of it," he said with a shrug. "What else can I do? What else can anyone do? And there's plenty to be grateful for. There almost always is. But those questions… there aren't any answers. No guarantees, except that life goes on, and maybe, just maybe, there's a greater purpose in it somewhere, if you believe. But the made-to-order happy ending? Those don't exist."

"Don't they?" Laurel said. "I want them to."

"I think everyone does, but you've got to do the best with what you're given."

"What if it's not enough?" she asked, a bit desperately. "What if it won't make you happy?"

"Then you need to think about why it won't, I suppose.

Perhaps happiness is right there all along, and you just haven't seen it."

"Yes, but…" It felt a little too make-do-or-mend for Laurel's taste, and yet she realised how naïve and passive it was to think a happy ending was just going to fall into her lap. Not that she thought that, exactly, and yet…

And yet what?

Laurel didn't even know. Her head was spinning, but at least the threat of having a major wobbly was receding. The pressure in her chest and the thickness in her throat had both eased, thank goodness. Laurel felt composed enough to turn to Archie and give him what she hoped passed for a rueful smile.

"Thank you, Archie. You're right, of course. I don't know why I'm having such a wobble now. But I think you've talked me down from the ledge."

"I don't think you were quite that far gone," Archie returned with a smile. "Coming back here was tougher than you expected it to be. I can understand that. Memories are powerful things. So are dreams, and it sounds like you've got a lot of both."

"Yes…" With a jolt of awareness, Laurel realised how close he was. She breathed in the bay rum scent of his aftershave and it made her dizzy. Their shoulders were brushing, their breath mingling, and then Archie was leaning even closer, angling his head down towards her while Laurel's mind emptied out and she froze where she stood, so, so conscious of his nearness—his pressed shirt, his shaven jaw, his hair which was starting to stick up again, in the front.

And then he did what some part of her brain had known and been expecting him to do all along. He kissed her.

Chapter Eleven

LAUREL'S BRAIN SHORT-CIRCUITED at the brush of Archie's lips against her own. His lips were cool and soft, the caress more like a question, and before she could process what was happening, or think about what she was doing or how she felt about it, she gave its answer.

Laurel jerked her head away from his and took a definitive step back, one hand pressed against her thumping heart.

They stared at each other for one endless, agonising moment, and a look of hurt vulnerability flashed across Archie's rugged features before he composed his face into the far more expected expression of easy affability.

"Sorry," he said. "That shouldn't have happened. I suppose I got carried away."

Laurel's face felt as if it was on fire, her heart was beating painfully hard, and she felt even nearer to tears than before. "No," she said. "It's not... I just..." She could not find the words. She didn't even know which ones she was looking for. She had no idea how she felt, or why she'd stepped away so quickly, and yet she had. She *had*.

Archie shook his head, smiling. "It's all right, Laurel. I understand."

Did he? Did *she*? "I'm sorry," Laurel said, one hand still pressed to her chest. Her heart was racing. "If… if…" Her tongue felt thick, the words coming clumsily. "If I gave out the wrong message somehow…" She thought of those cosy dinners, blabbing on about Mr Right, how she'd kept going to him for advice and comfort and company…

Of *course* she'd given out the wrong message. She felt both stupid and mean and *stupid*. So stupid.

"No, no, you didn't." Archie was still shaking his head. "Please don't worry about that. This is entirely on me. But let's say nae more about it. It was a moment, that was all, a foolish moment. Christmas, mistletoe, moonlight, and all that." Even if there was neither mistletoe nor moonlight in this moment. "Let's put it behind us," he said firmly. "For good. But I think I'd better go check on my dad." With a quick smile that didn't crinkle his eyes, he turned and walked back into the hotel.

Alone in the cold and dark, Laurel let out a sound that was part groan, part whimper, part howl. If only that hadn't happened. If only she hadn't jerked away like that, as if she'd been disgusted. Why had she? And yet what else could she have done? She'd enjoyed Archie's company these last few days, of *course* she had, but she couldn't ever think of Archie like that.

Could she?

He wasn't at all the man of her stupid, schoolgirl fantasies, not that that mattered. In that moment Laurel knew that was all they'd ever been… fantasies. She'd never really been expecting a Mr Darcy lookalike to emerge dripping from a pond, of course she hadn't.

But Archie? Archie MacDougall, a man who wore jumpers with more holes than wool, and talked to cookers, and made lemon drizzle cake, and spent his days with *sheep?* He was tied to this island, which was lovely but on the edge of nowhere, and a relationship between them, even if she'd wanted one, would never work.

But if Archie hadn't kissed her, they could have gone on being friends, if only for another week. Now Laurel feared it was all going to be terribly awkward, and there would be no more cosy suppers in Archie's kitchen, no games of Ludo or Monopoly, no comfortable chats as they washed the dishes… basically, Christmas was ruined, and worse, far worse, she might have ruined it for Archie.

She hated the thought of having hurt him, hated it with a ferocity that made her want to howl. He was far too nice a man for her to have done that. He was far too nice a man for her.

Swallowing hard, Laurel headed back inside. The band was taking a break and a buffet was being served on the side of the ballroom, although Laurel knew she couldn't manage a mouthful. Her stomach swirled with nerves and the acidic aftertaste of disappointment.

She looked around for Archie, but she didn't see him anywhere, and when she glanced into the foyer, she saw the receptionist watching *Elf* all alone. Had Archie taken his dad and just *left?* Her stomach seethed even more, and forcing herself forward, she went to look for Zac. He was standing with a few lads his own age; they were tossing cocktail sausages into each other's mouths and laughing loudly whenever one of them succeeded in catching one.

Laurel didn't want to spoil their fun, but she felt rather desperate to go back to Bayview Cottage and crawl beneath her duvet. Still, for Zac's sake, she turned away, and decided to get another drink. A glass of wine this time.

She took her large glass of pinot grigio to a quiet corner of the room, wanting only to sip it in silence, her mind still twisting and turning on itself, with no real answers to the questions seething in it. *Why did Archie have to kiss her? Was everything going to be ruined? Why did she feel quite so upset? What would happen now?*

"Hello, you look new." A fortyish woman with red hair and a wide smile came up to Laurel, forcing her to smile back even though everything in her protested.

"Yes, I am."

"Visiting family, or…"

"Sort of. My aunt Eilidh lives outside Stromness, and I'm staying in her cottage."

"Eilidh Campbell?" Laurel nodded. "How lovely. I know her well."

"It seems as if everyone knows everyone around here."

"Yes, well, we're a close-knit community." The woman smiled comfortably. "My name's Emma, by the way."

"Laurel."

"You're here with your son?" She cast an eye around the room and then nodded towards Zac, who was still with the others, throwing cocktail sausages into each other's mouths.

"My nephew, actually. My sister's son." Laurel left it at

that, not wanting to explain, and Emma let it go.

"And you know Archie? I saw the two of you chatting..." There was a gleam in Emma's eye that made everything in Laurel tense. This was a close-knit community indeed.

"I know him a little. He takes care of Eilidh's cottage, and Zac, my nephew, has been helping out on the farm while we're here." She spoke repressively, not even meaning to, but Helen clocked her tone and nodded.

"I see."

And Laurel thought she probably saw too much, although she didn't even know what there was to see, all things considered.

"Archie's lovely," Emma continued. "I've always thought it a shame that he never settled down."

Hoo boy. Laurel could see where this was going. And even though she knew she shouldn't, Laurel couldn't help asking, "Why do you think that was?"

Emma's eyes gleamed brighter, now that Laurel had taken the bait. "I don't rightly know. He's tied to the farm, of course, and the island. And his father... you know about his father?"

Laurel nodded, which of course only added to Helen's speculation. "He has a lot of commitments, I suppose. And the farming life is a hard one, nonstop."

"Yes, but surely there are women who are willing to sign up for that." Not that she was one of them, although part of her wondered suddenly why she was so certain she wasn't.

"You'd think so, wouldn't you," Emma agreed with a shrug. "He's had a few dates over the years, but no one special, as far as I know. Perhaps that will change." She raised her eyebrows hopefully, and Laurel glugged the rest of her wine.

"I hope so, for his sake," she said in as non-committal a tone as she could manage. "I need to get Zac home." Even if it wasn't yet ten o'clock. For Laurel, the party had definitely ended.

She was silent as they walked back to Bayview Cottage, her mind still in turmoil. For Zac's sake, she decided to try to make conversation, and asked about the friends he'd made.

"They're okay," Zac said with a shrug. Laurel deemed that high praise; Zac was never one to gush. He turned to her, his gaze narrowed. "Are you all right, Aunt Laurel?"

Laurel nearly stumbled in her surprise. Zac had never asked her a question like that before. "Of course I am," she said automatically. "Why do you ask?"

He shrugged, his hands jammed into the pockets of his jeans. "I don't know. You just seem, like, well stressed."

Well stressed? Laurel got the gist if not the grammar. "I'm not," she protested, and Zac gave her a look.

"Whatever you say," he said, sounding utterly unconvinced.

Back at the cottage, Laurel made a cup of hot cocoa and took it to bed, huddling under the duvet and still feeling miserable. She thought about ringing Soha, but she couldn't without Wi-Fi or phone signal, and in any case she knew what Soha would say. *If you regret brushing him off, then just go for it the next time you see him. What have you got to lose?*

And really, what *did* she have to lose? Except maybe her dignity if Archie rejected her…

And yet she was incredibly reluctant to take such a risk. There couldn't be any future for them. Her life was in York. Archie was rooted in Orkney. And, really, this was *Archie*. Did she—could she—feel that way about him? She didn't even know, and yet the thought of losing his friendship…

Laurel let out a groan as she pulled the duvet over her head, as if she could block out the world. The trouble was, she didn't know what she wanted. The dream that might never happen, or the reality that felt too scary and uncertain and well, *real*?

The questions were still pinging around her brain like balls in a pinball machine when she fell into a restless doze, only to wake as sunlight filtered through the crack in the curtains, which meant it already had to be after nine o'clock. A tapping on her door had her sitting up, blinking sleep out of her eyes, her hair sticking up more than Archie's and her voice a croak.

"Yes…"

"Aunt Laurel? I brought you a coffee."

What? Had Zac had a personality transplant? Or was this the sweet kid she'd always hoped lurked beneath the sullen façade?

"Thanks, Zac. Come in."

He came in hesitantly, almost shyly, thrusting the cup of coffee at her which Laurel took with grateful hands. All right, he'd definitely not used enough milk, and there were grounds swimming in it, but still. It felt like the best cup of coffee she'd ever had.

"Thank you, Zac. That was really kind of you."

He hunched one shoulder. "'S nothing."

It wasn't, but Laurel knew better than to make a big deal of it and embarrass him. "Thanks," she said again, and took a sip, trying not to wince at the taste of it. Way too weak, and also way too much sugar.

"Are you okay?" Zac asked, and Laurel thought she heard a hint of vulnerability in his voice that made her ache. It occurred to her how uncertain Zac's world was—his mother in rehab, excluded from school, his only guardian seeming as if she were having a major wobbly.

"Zac, I'm fine," Laurel said firmly. "You don't need to worry about me."

He gave her a look bordering on disgust. "I'm not worried."

"Of course you're not," Laurel answered as she hid a smile behind her cup, risking another sip of coffee. "Sorry."

"It's just, you haven't, like, fallen out with Archie, have you?"

Her fingers tightened on the cup. "No. Why do you ask?"

"I don't know. He left kind of quickly last night, and then you seemed a bit, well, off."

Yes, she'd definitely been off. "We haven't fallen out." She hoped.

"He's a nice guy, you know, if…" Zac shrugged, his gaze sliding away.

"Yes, he's very nice," Laurel said, meaning for it to be the end of the conversation. She wasn't about to take dating advice from a fourteen-year-old.

Zac gave her a slightly pitying look. "You could do worse, you know," he said, and sloped off, back to his bedroom.

She could do worse. How damning for both her and Archie, who probably seemed like two old geezers to Zac. They sort of were.

Laurel put all thoughts of Archie firmly to the back of her mind as she rose from the bed, made herself a proper cup of coffee, drinking it in secret in case she hurt Zac's feelings, and then showered and got dressed. It was Christmas Eve, and she had a lot to do.

She blasted bagpipe carols as she finished wrapping her presents, and Zac rather nonchalantly told her he was going to walk into Stromness and have a look around. Laurel suspected he was going to buy her a present, and it made her smile as she just as nonchalantly agreed that he could.

She prepped as much of tomorrow's roast dinner as she was able, and debated walking over to Archie's to check that he was okay to come round tomorrow. It would be better, she decided, to clear the air before they saw each other on Christmas Day, and so she left a note for Zac and headed once more across the paddock.

When she arrived at the farmhouse, however, it was clearly empty. Archie's mud-splattered Rover wasn't in the farm yard, and everything was dark and closed up, which made her feel inexplicably sad. Even the dogs were gone, or at least they didn't set up a chorus of barking the way they normally did.

Laurel stood there for a moment, feeling the emptiness all around her, and then she scribbled a note, reiterating her invitation for tomorrow, and pushed it under Archie's door, hoping he'd catch sight of it as he came in.

Knowing there was nothing more she could do, she turned from the empty farmhouse and walked back across the frost-tipped fields, under a leaden sky.

That evening she and Zac walked into Stromness for a Christmas Eve service at the parish kirk, which had been billed as mince pies, mulled wine, and Christmas carols from half past ten in the evening to midnight, something Laurel was looking forward to despite her lingering sadness over things with Archie.

"Did you ever go to a Christmas service with your mum?" she asked as they walked through the quiet streets, the Christmas lights casting a colourful glow on the rain-slicked pavements.

"Nope."

"This is your first one?"

"I did a nativity in primary school."

"That doesn't count."

Zac gave her a look.

"Christmas Eve is special," Laurel insisted. She thought of what Archie had said—about Christmas being the right time for miracles.

Was she still waiting for a miracle? For magic? And was it hopeless if she was?

Laurel stepped into the church, breathing in the dusty,

faded smell of stacks of hymnals and candle wax, mixed with the spicy scent of evergreen and mulled wine.

"Welcome, welcome!" A greeter at the door clasped both her hands in his. "Come, get a cup of mulled wine and a mince pie. We're so glad you're here."

Laurel couldn't help but smile back, charmed by his genuine warmth, and murmured that she was glad she was here, as well.

Soon she and Zac were sitting in a surprisingly comfy pew, nibbling mince pies. A string quartet was playing quietly before the service officially started, and the church was decked with evergreen and Advent candles. It was so peaceful that Laurel felt herself relax, the uncertainties and tensions she'd been carrying around for the last few weeks, and especially since Archie had kissed her, starting to slip away.

Then the service began, with a rousing rendition of "Hark the Herald Angels Sing." Laurel loved Christmas carols, the innate and infectious joy of them, and she sang along, her heart lifting with every lyric.

"Light and life to all He brings, Risen, with healing in His wings," she sang with gusto, as Zac looked at her slightly askance. He was merely mouthing the lyrics, but even that was something.

Light and life. Healing. She let the words, the promises, reverberate through her. Those were things she'd always wanted, things she'd been waiting to happen, like presents to be unwrapped. But what if that wasn't how it happened, after all?

What if the magic, the *miracle*, wasn't like a bolt from the sky, a shot in the dark, something she had to wait and wait for, until everything was made perfect?

What if the miracle was, as Archie said, found here and now, in the midst of the confusion and brokenness, the hurt and disappointment? What if the miracle was found in the moment, with all it held, rather than on some distant day?

She didn't have to force it. She didn't have to find it. It was already there.

The thought was so novel, so strange and unexpected, that Laurel didn't know what to do with it. But as she sang "Silent Night" and the lights dimmed in the church to a few flickering candles, everyone's voice an expectant, joyful near-whisper, she felt as if she were, perhaps for the first time, on the cusp of something wonderful.

As the last chorus fell away to a reverent hush, she turned to Zac and smiled, and felt the miracle begin to unfold as he smiled back.

Chapter Twelve

LAUREL WOKE ON Christmas morning to a sense of expectation and a light dusting of snow on the ground.

"Snow!" she called to Zac joyfully, and he ran into her bedroom to look out the window with her at the tufty grass leading down to the sea, all of it sparkling white, if only just.

"It'll probably melt by lunchtime," he said, and Laurel laughed out loud.

"But it's here now." She reached for her dressing gown. "Let's go downstairs." Last night, after Zac had gone to bed, she'd filled his stocking with the sweets and treats she'd bought in town, and she was looking forward to him opening it all, although she felt a bit apprehensive, too. What if Zac didn't really *get* Christmas? What if he turned his nose up at a Rubik's cube or a Terry's chocolate orange? Well, she told herself, then so be it. It didn't have to be the end of the world.

When she came downstairs, however, she was the one who was surprised, not Zac. For next to his red felt stocking, stuffed with goodies, was her own, also filled.

"What..." Laurel stared at in incomprehension. "How..." She'd bought herself a stocking, but then she'd put it in a kitchen drawer, not wanting to put any pressure on Zac to get her presents. She didn't even know if he had money. And yet here was her stocking, and she could see a Kendal mint cake sticking out of the top, which was her favourite sweet. *How...?*

"Did you do this?" she asked, almost accusingly, and Zac nodded with sheepish pride.

"Yeah, Archie and I drove into Kirkwall one afternoon, after we'd finished at the farm. But I bought it all," he added quickly. "With the money I earned."

"Oh, Zac." Laurel sniffled, suddenly near tears.

"Don't cry," he warned, sounding alarmed. "It isn't much. Just some sweets and stuff."

"But it was so thoughtful of you. Thank you." He shrugged, and she smiled, and then they both dove into their stockings, exclaiming over the small yet thoughtful gifts—a new hair clip for Laurel, as she'd broken one a few days ago, and some hair gel for Zac, because she'd seen he'd run out.

It was the small things that counted, Laurel realised as she bit into her mint cake. The tiny things that told her someone had noticed and cared.

After they'd finished opening their stockings, Laurel made hot chocolate and put the cinnamon buns she'd prepped the night before into the Rayburn, so soon the whole cottage was filled with the spicy, yeasty scent. They ate the rolls and sipped their hot chocolate while still in their pyjamas, gazing out at the snow-covered sheep paddock between Bayview Cottage and Archie's farmhouse. The snow hadn't even started to melt yet, despite the sun rising over the fields to the east, the sky a perfect, pure blue.

After breakfast, they both showered and dressed, and Laurel started getting dinner ready while Zac tried to beat the world record on his new Rubik's cube. They'd agreed to wait to open presents until Archie came over, although Laurel felt apprehensive about it all.

She wasn't sure he really would come, or if she should give him the presents she'd bought, which felt too intimate now that he'd kissed her and she'd backed off. Still, Zac wanted to wait for Archie, and so for his sake as much as her own she wrapped Archie's presents and put them under the tree with the others.

By three o'clock Laurel was starting to feel antsy. When they'd initially discussed it, Archie had said Christmas dinner at the nursing home would finish by half past two, and he'd come right after.

Christmas dinner—Archie's second—was simmering and bubbling away, ready to be served by four o'clock. The presents, in their sparkly, festive paper, looked accusingly at her from under the little, lopsided tree. Zac had figured out the Rubik's cube and moved on to flicking through the "Four Thousand Facts You Need to Know" book Laurel had hoped he might like, which he seemed to, judging from the random facts he threw her way as she morosely prodded the carrots boiling away on top of the Rayburn.

"Did you know that in 2009, a search for the Loch Ness monster located 100,000 golf balls under the water?"

"And no monster? Goodness, that's a lot of golf balls."

Zac buried his nose back in his book. "And you can zip

wire from Spain to Portugal."

"Wow."

Zac put his book down. "When is Archie coming?"

Laurel felt as if her heart were twisting within her. What if she'd set Zac up for hurt yet again, another adult disappointing him? No dad, a mum in rehab, an aunt who had never been around. No wonder he'd bonded with Archie. But what if Archie didn't come... because of her? What if this was all her stupid fault?

And then, like another miracle, there was a tap-tap-tap on the door, and Zac went to answer it, and then Archie was coming in with a gust of cold air, his cheeks reddened by the wind, his hair sticking up the way it always did, despite his obvious attempts to tame it.

"Happy Christmas!" He clapped a hand on Zac's shoulder and smiled at Laurel from across the room. This one reached his eyes, and it was as if there had never been anything between them at all, and for a reason she couldn't fathom that made Laurel feel sadder than ever.

"Happy Christmas," she answered with a smile of her own. She didn't know if it reached her eyes or not. "You didn't have to bring anything..."

"Of course I did."

There was a lemon drizzle cake, homemade of course, a bottle of whisky liqueur, a box of gourmet chocolates, and a set of six Christmas crackers with whistles inside. Plus a bag of wrapped presents that Archie deposited beneath the tree before returning to the kitchen with a smile, his hands in his pockets.

He'd cleaned up nicely, Laurel noticed, again. He wore a pair of battered but serviceable cords in Christmas green and a maroon jumper that had only one hole in the elbow that Laurel didn't think he'd noticed.

"You're so kind to bring all this," she murmured, meaning it utterly.

"Thank you for having me."

"You've already had one Christmas dinner," she continued with a little laugh. "I'm not sure you want another…"

Archie patted his trim stomach. "Always room for more."

"Let's open presents first," Zac interjected, and Laurel glanced at Archie for affirmation.

"Sounds good to me."

They assembled in the little sitting room, made cosier with the Christmas lights on the tree and the fire burning down to embers in the grate.

Archie threw another log on it and stirred up the glowing embers, sending a few flames soaring higher. Zac threw himself on the sofa and Laurel stood in the doorway, taking it all in, her heart so full it almost felt painful. How had they got to this moment, the three of them, celebrating Christmas together?

Here was the miracle. Here was the magic. Her heart felt as if it might burst.

"Who's going to go first?" Zac asked, and Laurel took a deep breath as she came in to sit on one end of the sagging sofa, while Archie took a seat in the chair opposite.

"You can go first, Zac," she said.

Zac clearly had got the hang of this Christmas thing, for

he reached for the biggest box with his name on it and started tearing paper. Laurel exchanged a wry, laughing look with Archie as Zac finished with the paper and opened the box.

"Wow, new trainers!" He looked stunned at the sight of the pair of Adidas, which had been pricier than Laurel had expected but worth it, because she'd seen Zac had a hole in the toe of his current pair, yet he insisted on wearing them just about every day. "Thanks, Aunt Laurel."

"You're welcome."

"You go, Archie," Zac said, and nudged a small box towards him.

Archie looked surprised. "I wasn't expecting presents for myself…"

"We asked you for Christmas," Laurel interjected. "Of course we got you presents." Although she was as touched as Archie looked to be that Zac had bought something for Archie—a book of Scottish poetry, she saw, as Archie opened it.

"You mentioned you liked Robert Burns," Zac said in a half-mumble, ducking his head.

"So I did, lad. So I did." Archie flicked through the book, looking moved. "And my mum did, as well," he said, and gave Zac a smile as well as another clap on the shoulder. "Thank you kindly, Zac."

"Now you, Aunt Laurel." Zac reached for a present Laurel didn't recognise and handed it to her. She read the tag— *To Laurel, From Archie*, and her heart flip-flopped.

"You shouldn't have…" she murmured.

"Enough of that, all right?" Zac interjected. "We all got each other presents. End of."

"All right," Laurel said with a laugh, and opened the present. It was a copy of *Pride and Prejudice*—a special, limited edition with illustrative plates and a biography of Jane Austen at the end. "Oh, Archie." She felt a lump forming in her throat.

"You've probably read it, but I thought you might like it, although it doesn't have Colin Firth," he said with a smile.

"I don't want Colin Firth." Laurel knew how daft she sounded, but she meant it utterly. She didn't want Colin Firth; she didn't want the stupid dream she'd always known as a fantasy, nothing more. Even so, how could she not have seen it before? She wanted this man right in front of her, with his crinkly eyes and messy hair and holey jumper. Yes, she wanted him. Just him, exactly as he was. But what if it was too late?

She swallowed hard and looked down at the book, tracing the elegant, raised lettering with her fingers. "Thank you," she said quietly. "This was very thoughtful."

"It's my turn again," Zac said, breaking the moment if there had even been one, and then he was opening a pair of waterproof plus fours from Archie, which he proclaimed were "ace", and then Archie was opening the cookbook she'd bought him, and already reading it avidly when Laurel opened a present from Zac.

"Archie helped me pick it out," he said. "It's from him, too."

"Now I'm really curious." Laurel opened the lumpy,

wrapped object, and as she pulled away the paper, she saw what it was—a snow globe of the waterfront in Stromness—the hotel, the harbour, the Christmas tree. When she turned it upside down, glittery snowflakes filled the scene and then settled.

"*Oh…*"

"To remember Orkney," Archie supplied quietly, and there was such a sadly wistful note to his voice that Laurel couldn't speak.

"It's lovely," she said after a long moment. "Thank you, Zac. And Archie." She couldn't look at Archie, afraid she might start to cry or even seriously sob. Or maybe grab him by his collar and kiss him, because she knew now that was what she really wanted to do, what she'd been wanting to do all along.

I made a mistake, she realised. *I made a stupid, childish mistake, and I don't know how to make it better.* Of course, she could just tell Archie so, but the thought of being so vulnerable, laying it all out there for him to walk away from, made everything in her cringe and curl up in fear.

She couldn't do that. She *never* did that, Laurel realised with a thrill of shocked comprehension. She surrounded herself with friends, and cats, and cosy crocheted throws, and called it a life because she was afraid—*terrified*—of the real deal. Loving someone. Letting them in. Letting them see *her*, with all her quirks and fears and scars.

Because loving someone meant they left—first her mother, then Abby. Even her dad, in a way, retreating after her mother's death so their relationship had been based on a history of affection rather than the real thing, active and present.

No, she couldn't do that again. The horror with which she contemplated such a thing made Laurel realise just why she'd loved her dream so much. Because it was just a dream, and as long as dreams stayed dreams, they were safe. They couldn't leave. They couldn't hurt her. *That* was why she'd stepped away from Archie after he'd kissed her; why her boyfriends had never made it past the fourth or fifth date. Why, at thirty-five, she was still alone.

Because loving someone was the scariest thing you could ever do.

"Laurel?" Archie's voice was gentle. "You all right, lass?"

"Yes." Laurel cleared her throat and put the snow globe carefully on the mantle. She still didn't dare looking either of them in the eye. "Yes, I'm fine. Zac's turn now."

Zac opened a hoodie Laurel had bought him, with Orkney on the front, and exclaimed over it, and then Archie opened the jumper she'd bought him, exclaiming over it more than Zac had his hoodie, and Laurel blushed and mumbled something about all his jumpers having too many holes.

"But you should have another present," Zac said. "You got two for me, and for Archie..."

"Oh, I love giving presents," Laurel said quickly. "Don't worry about me. I should check on our dinner, though." She lurched up from the sofa, catching Archie's concerned frown out of the corner of her eye, before she hurried to the kitchen. "Dinner's almost ready," she called, sounding, she feared, a bit manic. "I'll get it all on the table. Archie, why don't you set the crackers out?"

The next few minutes were a flurry of activity as they all worked together to get all the food—Laurel had made way too much—to the table, and then assembled there. Laurel hadn't looked anyone in the face once, yet she had to as they all sat down, and Laurel asked Archie to say grace.

He cleared his throat and began, "Be present at our table, Lord, be here and everywhere adored, and grant that we might feast in Paradise with Thee." He gave them both a self-conscious smile. "My dad's grace."

"I love it," Laurel said sincerely. "How is your dad?"

Archie shrugged. "Today wasn't one of his better days, unfortunately. He didn't really know what was going on, but he enjoyed his Christmas pudding."

Which meant, Laurel surmised, that he hadn't recognised his own son. Her heart ached once more for Archie, for all of it. All the losses and secret sorrows and missed opportunities. Could they move past them? Could she?

"Well, dig in, everybody," she said, and passed the platter of fluffy Yorkshire puddings.

Dinner was, thankfully, both delicious and enjoyable. Laurel had been afraid that with this new, emotional hyperawareness of Archie, she might make a fool of herself, but she thought she acted fairly normally, and she'd made herself meet his eye several times over the course of the meal.

After they'd eaten, they got the whistles from their Christmas crackers, and with the help from the music sheet that came with the box of crackers, they whistled their way through several carols, dissolving into helpless laughter several times at the cacophony they were making.

"This is actually worse than the bagpipe carols," Laurel said, and Archie looked surprised.

"Bagpipe carols? I have that CD."

Laurel met Zac's gaze and they both burst out laughing again. Laurel didn't want any of it to end; she couldn't remember feeling so happy, so truly content, even in the midst of her own tangled emotions, that buzzing awareness. Why had she never noticed how truly fit Archie was? His physique was both sinewy and strong, and Laurel didn't think she'd seen anything sexier than Archie with his shirt-sleeves rolled up over his strong, tanned forearms. She kept staring at them, at him.

Of course the evening had to end; Zac helped clear the table before sloping off to play a game on his phone—he'd been device-free all day so Laurel could hardly blame him.

But it meant that she and Archie were alone, with an almighty pile of dirty dishes, and she didn't know if she was brave enough to say something about how she felt.

"You wash, I dry?" he asked lightly, which was their usual. Laurel nodded, and they set to it, standing side by side, the only sound the clink of cutlery and the clank of plates.

"This has been a lovely Christmas," Archie said after a moment. "Far better than my usual."

"Far better than mine, as well," Laurel answered. So, *so* much better.

"Really? I thought you had a passel of friends back in York you celebrated with."

"Hardly a passel, however many that means." She handed a wet, rinsed plate to Archie, their fingers brushing, sending a twang of awareness through her. "And not every Christmas. People usually have plans. Family, boyfriends or girlfriends, exotic holidays."

"I suppose you could count this as an exotic holiday," Archie said with a laugh.

"Yes..." Suddenly Laurel felt breathless. She couldn't bear another second of this chitchat, easy as Archie made it seem. She just couldn't. She had to be brave enough now. She *had* to.

She turned to him so fast her head spun, and her heart was already pounding. "Archie..."

He was standing close to her, close enough for her to see the tiny flecks of gold amidst the blue in his eyes, to see where he'd nicked his jaw shaving, and where a twist of greying hair stuck up behind his ear. He frowned, eyebrows lowering.

"Laurel..."

Laurel took a deep breath. She clenched her fists still wrist-deep in the soapy water, and then she leaned forward and pressed her lips to Archie's. They were cool and soft, just as they'd been before, and they were very still beneath hers. Too still.

Archie put one hand on her shoulder, and not in a good way. He didn't take that awful step back the way she had, but the message was just as clear. *Not this.*

Laurel drew back a little, afraid to look him in the face, but she made herself do it. He was smiling at her sadly, his eyes crinkled in concern. Not the passionate, tender look she'd been hoping for.

"I'm sorry, Laurel."

Oh, no. Heat flooded her face and mortification her soul. And worse, far worse, *hurt.* Hopeless, heart-breaking hurt. She tried for a smile but her lips just trembled. "So you really did just get carried away at the ceilidh, huh?" she managed in a voice that sounded both croaky and shrill.

Archie was silent for a moment, his expression thoughtful as he gazed at her full in the face. "No," he said at last. "I didn't get carried away, not like that."

"But…"

"I don't want your pity, Laurel. I don't need some—some sort of compensation kiss." His Scottish brogue had got thicker with the force of his emotion, making Laurel strain to understand him.

"*Compensation…*"

"Don't feel sorry for me," he practically growled. "For whatever reason. Because I'm a barmy, middle-aged farmer with a dad who doesn't remember me and aught but sheep for company. I kissed you at the ceilidh because I meant it, but I don't want to be kissed back like a favour."

Laurel goggled at him for a few seconds as her mind raced to keep up with what he was saying. "You *are* a barmy, middle-aged farmer," she finally managed, "but I wasn't kissing you as a *favour*. I kissed you because I wanted to, Archie MacDougall, and I've been wanting to since *you* kissed *me*."

"But you backed off—"

"I was stupid," Laurel said fiercely. "Stupid and scared.

I've regretted it ever since. I've been seriously out of sorts since that night. Ask Zac. He'll tell you."

Archie shook his head slowly. "Laurel..."

"I want to kiss you," she said again, feeling both reckless and ridiculous in stating such a fact. "A lot. Do you want to kiss me?"

Archie stared at her for a moment, and then he gave her his answer. He cupped her face in his big, callused hands, running his thumb over her lower lip, making Laurel's insides shiver, and then he kissed her. Properly.

A kiss that made her heart do somersaults and her stomach feel like a bowl of jelly, and her back knifed into the counter as Archie pressed into her and they kissed and kissed until the world felt like that snow globe, with glittering snow all around them, and nothing else mattered but this.

They broke apart when the doorbell rang, more of a wheeze than anything else, and Laurel blinked stupidly at Archie, her lips buzzing, her heart singing, while he blinked just as stupidly back.

"Who..." she began.

Archie took a step back, raking a hand through his hair, making it stick up even more than it usually did. "You'd better answer that."

Laurel practically tottered to the door; her legs felt as wobbly as a newborn foal's, and her lips were *still* buzzing. She pressed her fingers to them, laughing softly to herself, as she opened the door, half-expecting a caroller, or perhaps someone who needed directions, or a kindly neighbour she'd never met. But no, it wasn't anyone like that.

"Hello, Laurel," Abby said.

Chapter Thirteen

L AUREL STARED DUMBLY at her sister for a few seconds
while her mind whirred emptily. Abby was wearing an
expensive-looking parka, with a cashmere cardigan underneath, and a pair of skinny jeans that were clearly haute
couture. She looked elegant and sophisticated and also
exhausted.

"Abby," Laurel said faintly. "How did you…"

"It wasn't easy. There aren't any ferries running on
Christmas Day. I had to hire someone to take me privately,
and leave my car in Scrabster."

"Come in," Laurel said belatedly, and stepped aside so
her sister could come into the cottage.

Abby walked in, glancing around in a way that reminded
Laurel how shabby the place was. "I haven't been here in
forever," Abby said in a distant voice. "Not since Mum…"

"I know. Me neither." Laurel was still having trouble
grasping the fact that her sister was actually here. "Did you
drive all this way…"

"I flew to Inverness, and then rented a car."

"You could have called—"

"I did, and left several voicemails. You didn't respond,

but from your surprise, I suppose you haven't had any signal?"

Laurel shook her head. "Sorry." She hadn't even glanced at her phone in days, so she wouldn't have seen if Abby had called, anyway. "I thought you were still in rehab..." she ventured uncertainly.

"I checked myself out."

"You can do that?"

"It's not a prison, Laurel." Abby sounded both defensive and irritable. "I checked myself in, I can check myself out."

"Right. Sorry."

"Where's Zac?"

Of course Abby wanted to see her son. "He's upstairs..." And Archie was in the kitchen.

"How is he?" Abby asked, biting her lip, suddenly looking wretched.

"He's okay." Laurel felt cautious. Did Abby want to hear that her son was doing all right without her, or that he wasn't? "Do you want to go up to him? I can give you some space..."

Abby bit her lip harder, her teeth sinking in deep enough to draw blood. "I've made such an absolute mess of things," she said in a low voice.

"It's not too late, Abby." For what, Laurel didn't even know. But she felt it strongly, that it *couldn't* be too late. Not for Abby and Zac, maybe not even for Abby and her. Another miracle, messy and complicated, but still. A miracle. "Why don't you go up and talk to him?"

Abby glanced fearfully at the stairs, and then nodded.

"All right. I will."

Laurel watched her mount the stairs before turning to the kitchen, everything feeling surreal, as if she was in a film, and someone with a camera was going to jump out and yell surprise.

Archie had finished the washing up, and was just hanging a tea towel on the Rayburn's railing when Laurel came into the kitchen.

"My sister is here," she said numbly. "I can't believe it."

"I gathered that's who it was."

"She's with Zac now. I don't even know… I don't know anything." She looked at him helplessly. "What happens now?"

Of course Archie didn't have the answer. "I should give you all some space," he said, and Laurel watched as he gathered his things—his presents, his coat. They hadn't even had pudding, which they'd been saving for after the washing up, or coffee, or the whisky liqueur, or anything. Laurel had been looking forward to the whole evening—games by the fire, maybe a movie later, and definitely another kiss.

She wanted to revel in the kiss she and Archie had already shared, the most astonishingly wonderful kiss of her life, not that there had been that many, but right then it felt as if it hadn't even happened. Archie was putting on his coat.

"Archie…"

"I really should go," he said. Now he was the one not meeting her eyes. Laurel felt as if all the hope and happiness that had been enveloping her in a warm bubble had just popped. *Splat.*

"You don't have to..." she began, because she really didn't want him to go, even as she recognised the sense of it in this moment.

"You need your space. Abby will want to talk to you, as well."

"Yes, but I don't even know what she wants." Laurel almost suggested that she come back to the farm with Archie, but she wasn't brave enough to suggest it, not when he was looking as if he couldn't get out of there fast enough.

"She'll tell you, I'm sure." His hand was on the knob of the back door.

"When will I see you again?" Laurel asked, hating how plaintive she sounded.

"I'll be around," Archie assured her. "You know where to find me."

"But..." That sounded so ambivalent, so non-specific. What if this was it? Panic fluttered inside her like a caged bird futilely beating its wings. This *couldn't* be the end. But with Abby here... and everything now so uncertain... what if Abby wanted to return to London? And even if she didn't want to go back right away, Laurel's life was still in York. Where exactly had she thought this was going?

"Okay," she said at last, and with a brief nod and an awful look of relief Archie opened the door and stepped outside. Laurel watched him loop around to the front of the cottage, and then she heard his car start up, and then he was gone.

She sank into a chair at the kitchen table, feeling as if she'd been shipwrecked on a foreign and desolate shore. She had no idea what to do, or even what to feel, now. She strained to hear Abby and Zac upstairs, and caught a low murmur, but nothing else.

What now? What on earth now?

In the end, Laurel didn't so much as move for about twenty minutes, letting her mind empty out as her body sagged. Then Abby came downstairs, pulling her cardigan around her slender body, her face haggard.

Laurel rose from her seat automatically. "Do you want a cup of tea? Or…" She couldn't think of anything else. Whisky liqueur? Chocolate?

"A cup of tea would be nice," Abby said. Laurel couldn't tell anything from her tone. "Do you have any herbal?"

"Er… no."

Abby sank into a chair at the opposite end of the table. "Oh, who am I kidding? Builder's brew is fine."

Laurel wasn't sure what to make of that comment, so she said nothing as she went to fill the kettle and switch it on. "How is Zac?" she finally worked up the courage to ask, as the kettle started to hum and Abby didn't move, her head propped by her hand, her gaze distant.

"I don't know." She glanced at Laurel. "He's being monosyllabic at the moment."

Laurel thought of Zac earlier in the day, laughing as he blew the whistle from his cracker, craning forward to see Archie open his present. It felt like a lifetime ago. In a way, it was.

"I've seen monosyllabic," she said finally. "He was monosyllabic for the first two weeks."

Abby's face contorted, and Laurel felt as if she'd said the wrong thing. "Thank you," she said flatly. "For taking care of him."

"I was glad to." There was so much more Laurel wanted to say, but she couldn't articulate it now, especially not when Abby had such a closed look on her face, and Zac was upstairs, and she had no idea what was really going on. The kettle clicked off and she spent the next few moments making cups of tea, the silence in the room starting to feel thick and oppressive.

"Abby," she finally said as she handed her sister a mug. "Are you... are you doing okay?"

Abby jerked her head up, her hands tightening on the mug. "Do I look okay?" she asked, and Laurel didn't know how to respond.

"Umm... sort of?" she ventured. "I love your cardigan."

Abby's lips twitched in a smile and then she turned away, her dark hair, the same colour as their father's, falling like a curtain in front of her face. "We need to go back to London as soon as possible."

Laurel's stomach tumbled towards her toes. "Why so soon? I mean, now that you're here..."

"Zac told me he's been excluded from school—"

"I left a message with the rehab centre—"

Abby waved her words aside. "I don't blame you. Of course I don't. But I need to find him a new school as soon as possible."

"But no schools will be open between now and New Year's," Laurel protested. She didn't want to go. She didn't want Zac and Abby to go. Couldn't they stay a few more days, at least?

"And I need to sort out work," Abby continued. "I took voluntary redundancy before I went into rehab."

"You did?" Laurel didn't really know what her sister did for work—something in finance that made loads of money.

"Yes, I did, and I need to figure out what I'm doing with my life."

And she needed to do that on Boxing Day, when all of the UK was closed down? Laurel swallowed down her protest. Her sister looked resolute.

And, she realised, just because Zac and Laurel were going back to London, didn't mean she had to leave... did it? For a few seconds she envisioned spending the week between Christmas and New Year's—Hogmanay, even—with Archie. Cosy evenings by the fire, kitchen suppers, time to get to know one another properly...

Then she remembered how hasty a retreat he'd beat just a short while ago. Who knew what was going to happen? And come New Year's, where would they both be? Laurel would go back to York; Archie would stay on Orkney. And there would be about five hundred miles between them.

"So when are you thinking of going?" she asked as the moments stretched on, the only sound the comforting rumble of the Rayburn and the drip of the tap.

"The day after tomorrow? I can't stomach driving all the way back tomorrow, but I don't want to be here any longer than that." Abby looked around the kitchen with something close to a shudder. "How can you stand it?"

"Stand it…"

"The memories."

Laurel looked at her in confusion. "But the memories are good here, Abby."

"Exactly."

"I don't understand…"

"Never mind." Her sister snapped the words out. "It doesn't matter. Zac and I are leaving the day after tomorrow."

And did that mean she was? Laurel struggled with how to talk to her sister in this mood—so closed-off, almost angry, definitely distant. Basically, the same as she'd been for the last twenty-five years. "Do you…" She hesitated. "Do you want me to come with you?"

Abby glanced at her sharply. "To London?"

"Er… yes? All I meant was, I can if you want me to." Why did she feel like she needed to apologise for offering? Was it out of place?

Abby looked away. "I… I don't know."

"I'm happy to help, Abby," Laurel said hesitantly. "Whatever you need… I know how you were always there, for me."

Abby's face contorted and she bit her lip. "Was I?" she asked, and Laurel didn't know how to answer. In any case, she didn't get a chance, because Abby drew herself up, assembling her chilly composure like the armour Laurel now suspected it was. "Anyway. I'm sure we'll be fine. I don't want to inconvenience you any more than I have…"

Abby stopped suddenly, her face crumpling, so Laurel

nearly went over and put her arms around her, even though she couldn't remember the last time she'd hugged her sister. Certainly not since she'd been a child.

"Abby…"

"Oh Laurel, everything is such a *mess.*" Abby put her hands up to her face, drawing in several gulping sort of breaths. "I've made such an utter mess of my life."

"Let me help," Laurel said quietly. "Please."

Abby took another gulping breath. "Okay. Yes. If you could come with us, even if just for a few days, that would might be… that would be great. Thank you."

"Okay." And as happy as she was that her sister was accepting her help, Laurel couldn't keep from feeling a sweep of loss. She would be leaving Orkney the day after tomorrow. Leaving Archie. And where did that leave them?

Abby went up to bed a few minutes later, and Laurel drifted around the downstairs, tidying the kitchen and putting presents away. She thought about checking on Zac, but it no longer felt like her prerogative, and in any case his bedroom door remained firmly closed all evening.

In the end she went up to her bedroom, feeling both disconsolate and hopeful. She was glad Abby was back in her life, but at what cost.

Except maybe she was imagining that. Archie had left so quickly… maybe all they'd shared was a kiss and nothing more.

Sitting on the edge of her bed, the night dark and moonless outside—all the snow had melted, just as Zac had said it would—Laurel held the precious snow globe in her hand and gave it a little shake. Inside the globe, the glittering snow flew everywhere, obliterating the cosy village scene, and as it settled once more Laurel was left with the terrible feeling that this was all she had left of her beloved island.

Chapter Fourteen

"**I**'M NOT GOING."

Laurel paused on the stairs at the sound of Zac's strident voice.

"Zac." Abby sounded both tearful and exasperated. "We need to get back to London. To normality."

"I *like* it here."

"Which boggles my mind, but still. This isn't real, Zac."

Laurel bit her lip, wondering if she needed that reminder, as well. Over the last week it had felt incredibly real. Incredibly wonderful.

"Aunt Laurel and I were going to stay until New Year's," Zac insisted. "And there's no point going back now. The whole world is, like, *closed*. Why can't we stay, Mum?"

Laurel heard the slight wobble in Zac's voice, his carefully cultivated attitude of bored indifference blown away. Abby must have heard it too, because she sighed.

"Do you really like it here? This cottage is so—"

"I like it," Zac said firmly. Laurel smiled. "And I'm meant to be working at Archie's—"

"Archie? Who is Archie?"

"A neighbour," Zac said a bit sullenly. "I've been working on his farm for the last week."

Had it only been a week? It felt like so much longer. Laurel hesitated on the step, wondering if she should stop eavesdropping and come into the kitchen.

"You've been working on a farm?" Laurel couldn't tell if her sister sounded appalled or impressed. Perhaps both.

"Please, Mum. I don't want to go back yet."

"Fine." Abby sighed. "Three more days. But then we really have to go."

"Okay." Zac sounded both relieved and disappointed; three days wasn't much, but at least it was something. Laurel decided it was time to make herself known.

"Good morning." She came into the kitchen with a smile; Zac was shovelling Cocoa Pops into his mouth and Abby was nursing a cup of coffee by the Rayburn, looking elegant but wan.

"Good morning." Her smile was brittle. "Zac is insistent that we stay here a little longer, so we'll leave on the twenty-ninth, if that's okay by you?"

"Of course." How could it not be? No matter what she felt about Archie, and she wasn't even sure yet what, or at least how much, that was, Laurel knew her sister had to be her first priority. Their history, their relationship, the ties that had bound them for decades, were what mattered. Not a fledgling romance with someone she might never see again, as much as that thought hurt.

But, she realised, she still wanted—and needed—to see Archie. Talk to him. "Zac, are you helping out at the farm today? I can drive you, if you like." Laurel thought she sounded casual enough, but she didn't think she'd fooled Zac as he opened his mouth, closed it, and then nodded.

Laurel turned back to Abby, who was sipping her drink with that distant look on her face. "And then maybe, when I get back, we could do something? Go for a walk, or…" She let that thought trail off into nothingness.

After a long moment, too long really, Abby gave a little nod. That was something, at least. Laurel switched on the kettle, deciding she needed a hit of caffeine before she faced Archie and said—what? She didn't even know.

Fifteen minutes later, they were driving down the bumpy, rutted track to Archie's farm. Laurel pulled into the yard to the accompaniment of a chorus of barking that made her both smile and ache. She had no idea what to expect when she walked into Archie's kitchen, except she was afraid she sort of did.

"Come on," she said to Zac, and they both climbed out of the Rover.

As they headed towards the back door, Zac suddenly veered off towards the barn.

"Um, I think I'll just go, uh, check on the animals."

"What?" Laurel frowned at him. "Zac…"

"For, like, twenty minutes or so?"

A blush warmed her cheeks as she realised what he was doing, and not very subtly. How much had Zac guessed or even seen between her and Archie last night? The thought made her blush harder.

"Okay," she said, trying to sound nonchalant and failing. "Thanks."

Zac mumbled a reply and hared off to the barn, leaving Laurel to gather her courage and head into the kitchen.

"Hello…" She poked her head through the door of the kitchen, but it was empty save for Aon, Dha, and Tri, who, after their initial bout of barking, had returned to their beds. Only one of them, Laurel didn't know which, raised his head from his paws before dropping it down again. They'd got used to her, Laurel realised, and the thought made her that unsettling combination of happy and sad.

"Where's your master, guys?" she asked as she stroked their heads in turn, and then, unsure what to do, filled up the kettle and plonked it on top of the Aga. "Where's he gone?" The kitchen had an empty, forlorn air—a pile of dirty clothes by the washing machine, a sink full of dirty dishes.

"I'm here." Archie appeared in the doorway, dressed in his usual barmy farmer get-up—plus fours, wax jacket, welly boots, flat cap. Laurel swallowed hard. "I was in the barn, and Zac said you'd come in here."

"Yes…"

"How is your sister?" He took off his flat cap and raked his fingers through his hair.

"I don't really know. We haven't talked much yet."

Archie nodded. "It will take time."

"Yes…" Why were they being so formal with one another? What had happened to the man who had cupped her face and kisses her breathless last night? Yet Laurel knew she wasn't brave enough to ask. She'd put herself out there last night already. She couldn't do it again, not when Archie was seeming so horribly polite. So she took her cues from him instead. "Thank you for everything yesterday." She sounded so stilted. "The presents, the chocolates… we haven't tried the whisky yet, but we will."

Archie just nodded.

"We're staying for another few days," Laurel blurted. "Until the twenty-ninth." She heard how hopeful she sounded, and it made her cringe, especially when Archie smiled sadly.

"Three days or thirty, Laurel," he said quietly. "Does it really make a difference?"

Her stomach felt as if it were freefalling. "What… what are you saying?"

Archie sighed heavily. "I'm saying that maybe last night we both got carried away."

Oh. Laurel tried to iron out the expression on her face, which she feared had become horribly crumpled. "Oh," she managed, her voice like a thread. "Right."

"It's just, we have different lives, don't we?" Archie lifted his shoulders in a what-can-you-do sort of shrug. "I can't leave Orkney, and you're in York."

"Yes. Of course." The words came automatically, and they reminded her of how she'd responded to her sister's brushoffs of old. *I'm busy, Laurel. I have to study. I can't come home.* And she'd always nodded and said, *yes, yes, of course. I understand.* Even when she hadn't, not really, not at all. But if she pretended she did, then maybe she wouldn't feel so hurt.

Except of course she had.

"Even if we were interested in having a—a relationship,"

Archie continued, "I don't see how it could work, with five hundred miles between us."

Even if? Did that mean he wasn't? What on earth could she say now? Then Laurel realised, with a sickening rush of disappointment, that there was nothing she could say to make this better.

Even if she wanted a relationship with Archie, how could she possibly pursue one now? She had Abby and Zac to think of. She was going to London with them, and she couldn't hare off to York or Orkney the minute her sister's back was turned, not when she was so vulnerable, her life so uncertain.

Besides, those five hundred miles meant a lot. She could hardly suggest moving to Orkney for Archie's sake, not when they barely knew each other, and did she really want to leave her whole life in York for a man she'd met last week?

And yet it all felt so unfair. Wrong, even. This wasn't the way it worked out in the movies, or those blasted BBC adaptations. Fantasies they might have been, but she could do with a small dose of it now.

"It's difficult," she managed at last. "I have Abby to think of now."

"Of course you do. The last thing you want to do is hitch yourself to an old codger like me, not that you're even thinking that way." He let out an odd little laugh. "At the end of the day, it was just a kiss."

Just a kiss. Except it had been so much more… hadn't it? Cosy suppers, evenings playing games, heart-to-hearts like Laurel hadn't had with anyone else, ever. Could she really turn her back on all that?

Did she have a choice?

On the Aga, the kettle begun to hum and then whistle. Soon it was a screech, and yet neither of them moved or spoke. What was Archie waiting for? *What was she?*

"Yes," Laurel said at last. "Yes, it was just a kiss."

BACK AT BAYVIEW Cottage, her heart leaden inside her, Laurel tried to smile as she asked Abby if she wanted to go for a walk on the beach. She'd left Archie right after they'd both agreed that all they'd shared was a kiss, and she felt as if she were dragging a two-ton weight around, each footstep an unbearable burden. Still, she had to try, with Abby, if not with Archie.

Archie. She couldn't think about him. Maybe one day she'd smile about her brief holiday romance, remember it with bittersweet whimsy, but right now it hurt far, far too much. It felt as if she were breaking into pieces inside, so her heart was nothing but flotsam, jagged pieces floating around in her body.

Still, Abby had agreed to a walk, and they headed through the garden to the beach, a stretch of silvery, damp sand under a heavy grey sky, the sea a flat surface stretching endlessly to the horizon.

"I forgot how bleak it is here," Abby remarked as they started walking along. "You really feel as if you're at the end of the world."

"I don't think it's bleak," Laurel protested, although she

supposed there was some truth to Abby's words—the vista of sea, sand, and sky, interspersed with tufty grass and jagged cliffs, was both bleak and beautiful. "Didn't you like it here, back when we were little?" she asked, steeling herself for the answer. Those memories were precious, but what if they weren't for Abby?

Abby sighed as she hunched deeper into her parka. "Of course I did. It felt magical."

"*Yes*—"

"But it ended."

"Yes," Laurel agreed cautiously, "but doesn't that make it more magical, in a way? More precious?"

Abby shook her head, seeming unwilling to say anything more. They walked in silence for a few moments, their boots squelching in the damp sand, and then Laurel finally risked another question.

"Abby, what made you go into rehab?"

Her sister let out a harsh laugh. "Why does anyone go into rehab?"

"Yes, but…"

"I was addicted to painkillers," Abby said flatly. She was staring straight ahead, her hands dug deep into the pockets of her parka. "I hurt my back a couple of years ago, and was prescribed Oxycodone. I kept taking the pills after I needed them, and then I started to buy them online."

"Painkillers," Laurel repeated faintly, her mind whirling.

"They took the edge off, softened everything that little bit. It was what I needed. But it got so one pill didn't do what I needed it to do, and so I started taking two, and then three with a glass of wine. It used to only be in evenings, but then I started at work. And you're not your sharpest, when the world is all beautifully blurry because you've taken so many drugs."

"So what happened?" Laurel whispered.

"The inevitable. A warning at work, and then an offer to take redundancy. They didn't want the embarrassment of having to fire me, and I had a nice boss who told me to get some help." She pressed her lips together, her expression turning hard, recriminating. "But it was Zac who made me go into rehab, not that he even knows it. After I took the redundancy, I went home and took three pills, washed down with a bottle of wine. Then I stopped breathing."

Laurel's mouth dropped open. "Oh, Abby…" *Oh, Zac.*

"He called 999, and fortunately I was okay. But I knew I couldn't let that happen again, ever, and so I checked myself into rehab the next morning. And told them to call you."

Laurel had so many more questions—why Abby needed to "take the edge off", as she said, and how could she help her sister now. How Zac was doing, and why things had gone wrong between them so long ago. So many, and yet she didn't know how to verbalise a single one.

"I'm so sorry that happened," she said at last. "So sorry."

Abby just nodded, grim-faced, and they kept walking, the silence between them not quite as tense, yet filled with so much they hadn't shared or said.

IN THE END, three days wasn't very long at all. Zac continued to work at the farm, and Abby slept, read, or occasionally went on walks with Laurel, although neither of them said very much.

Laurel felt the weight of all the things they hadn't yet said, things she knew they needed to talk about, but neither of them seemed willing or ready to begin. And she reminded herself not to force the issue—a bit of wisdom from Archie she was grateful to have—but to give Abby time, as well as herself.

And then the three days were gone, and Laurel was packing up their things, tidying the cottage back to its former emptiness, the life she'd lived here for ten short days as if it had never been.

She hadn't seen Archie once since she'd agreed with him that all they'd shared was a kiss—and yet what a kiss! But as she zipped up her suitcase, she felt the need to say goodbye, to have some sort of closure, if such a thing were even possible.

And so, the morning they were due to catch the ferry, she walked across the muddy paddock for the last time. Zac had already said goodbye, and was waiting morosely in the passenger seat of Abby's Rover, ready to go. Everything felt over.

The dogs set to barking as she reached the yard, and then Archie was at the door, a look of surprise flashing across his face before he gave her a cautious smile.

"I didn't expect you."

"I'm leaving this morning."

"I know. Zac told me."

"Of course."

They stared at each other for a long moment, and once again Laurel felt the weight of so much unspoken. It was too late to say any of it now, and yet she wanted to. She wanted him to know how much she cared.

"I'm going to London with Abby," she said. "Help her get back on her feet."

Archie nodded. "That's good."

"Yes. We still need to talk about—about things, but it's something."

Archie nodded again. He hadn't moved from the door, and Laurel couldn't bear to have to ask to come in. So she stood there, her hands in her pockets, the wind blowing her hair into tangles, feeling thoroughly miserable, wishing she were brave enough to tell him how much he meant to her.

"Anyway, I just wanted to say goodbye." Her throat was starting to thicken and she didn't have it in her to smile.

"That's kind of you."

"I wish…" Laurel began, and Archie raised his eyebrows. She smiled sadly, fighting tears. "I wish things were different, I suppose."

"Yes." Another one of his wretched nods. Then, gruffly, "Me too."

Laurel took a step towards him. "Archie…" But she didn't know what she was going to say, or if she could find the courage to say it, and Archie just waited, a look on his face that Laurel couldn't read. Coward that she was, she left it.

"I guess I'll go, then."

"All right."

No hug, then, and certainly no kiss. They simply stared at each other, two strangers again, minus the gun, but this felt far worse than their first meeting. Far, far worse.

"Goodbye, Archie," Laurel whispered, and then she turned and started walking back across the paddock, towards Bayview Cottage.

Half an hour later they were on the ferry, the island becoming no more than a dark green smudge on the horizon. Once on the mainland, they would pick up Abby's rental car and then drive to Inverness so she could return it, and then on to London. After that, who knew?

The hours passed in a rainy blur. As soon as they reached Thurso, Zac's phone signal flickered to life, and his thumbs started flying. Laurel watched him from the corner of her eye, feeling as if they were all reverting to their old ways, as if Orkney had never happened, and hating the thought.

"Zac," she said as she headed for the A9 towards Inverness, "how come you didn't want to go in the rental car with your mum?" He shrugged, a reply. "Zac... you're not... you're not angry with her, are you?" Another shrug. "I understand why you would be," Laurel said carefully, "at least in a way, but... she does love you. She's trying her best right now."

"Can we please not talk about this?" Zac asked in a suffocated sort of voice, his gaze firmly on his phone.

"Okay." She knew when not to push. "I just want things to be better," she said a bit lamely. "For everyone."

"It would be better if we'd stayed on Orkney."

And how. "Did you really like it that much there?" Laurel asked, and all she got was another shrug.

ABBY'S APARTMENT SMELLED stale—Laurel had forgot to empty the bin before leaving—and looked even more sterile than before, after the cosy shabbiness of Eilidh's cottage. Laurel could hardly believe they were all there.

After a meal of Indian takeaway—the hot curry managing to taste like ashes in Laurel's mouth—she got ready for bed, sleeping on an air mattress in Abby's living room. Zac had offered his bed, but Laurel had refused. She didn't want to turf her nephew out of his room, and in any case, his sheets had not been changed in some time.

Despite the endless day of travel, it took her hours to get to sleep, as a painfully bittersweet montage of moments of her time in Orkney ran through her mind on an endless loop, tormenting her with their poignancy. Laughing over Ludo with Archie and Zac… the clink of dishes as she and Archie washed up together… the lovely crinkle of his smile, his silly, tufty hair, the scorching kiss that had lit up every fibre of her being like a firework…

She eventually woke to a grey, misty dawn, the city shrouded in fog, and stumbled, body aching, from the bed to make herself a much-needed coffee.

To her surprise, Laurel saw Abby already sitting at the breakfast bar in the little kitchen.

"I didn't realise you were up…"

"Couldn't sleep," Abby said tightly, and Laurel nodded. "Me neither."

She went for the kettle, her fingers freezing on the switch, as Abby suddenly burst out, "Oh Laurel, why don't you hate me?"

And then her sister started to cry.

Chapter Fifteen

"I DON'T HATE you," Laurel said automatically. Her sister was crying quietly, shoulders shaking, tears streaming down her face, making no effort to compose herself. "Abby, I've never hated you."

"I've hated myself," Abby said through a hiccuppy sob. "For so long."

"Oh, Abby." Laurel sat on the stool next to her sister's, daring to lay a hand on her shoulder. She couldn't remember the last time they'd touched, but it felt right now. "Why?"

"*Why?*" Abby looked up at her, blinking through her tears. "Can you really ask me that?"

"You mean…" Laurel hesitated, feeling as if she were stumbling through the dark of her own ignorance. "Because of… me?"

Abby sniffled and nodded. "I just *left* you."

The words thudded through Laurel in a way she didn't expect. She hadn't realised until that moment how much she'd needed to hear Abby acknowledge that that was what had happened, that all the excuses she'd given and Laurel had accepted were just that. Excuses.

"Why?" she whispered. Now she was close to tears too,

swallowing hard and swiping at her cheeks to prevent a total breakdown.

Abby let out a long, raggedy sigh. "I never meant to, you know. I know that sounds cheap, but it's true. In a way, it just happened. At least at first."

"Tell me," Laurel instructed, because now they were here, actually talking about this stuff for the first time *ever*, she knew she needed to know. For her own peace of mind, and also for Abby's.

Abby drew a shuddering breath in an effort to compose herself. She wiped her cheeks and tucked her hair behind her ears, and then took a sip of tea, while Laurel waited, her heart starting to hammer.

"It was so hard after Mum died," she began quietly. "I know it was hard for you, too. Harder in some ways. You were so young. But for me..." She paused, pressing her lips together before blowing out a breath. "Dad just checked out," she said, her voice turning soft and sad. "I know he was never the most involved dad, but he was still *there*. You still felt he cared. But after Mum died..." Her face crumpled a bit before she smoothed it out into hard, determined lines. "I know he had his own grief. I understand that, I do. But he still had two daughters at home, one little, and one not as old as all that. And it was as if he didn't care about either of us."

"I don't remember," Laurel admitted sadly. The days and weeks after her mother's death were a blur of confusion and sadness, interspersed with happy moments she did remember—Abby taking her to Kinderland in Scarborough, her face sticky with candyfloss.

"I'm not surprised. Eight isn't that old, after all, and you'd only just had your birthday." Abby sighed. "But the truth is, it was affecting you. Dad was, with his distance. You didn't understand. And I couldn't stand that, so I tried to do stuff with you."

"Kinderland," Laurel said softly, and Abby nodded.

"Yes, we took the bus. I think you enjoyed that as much as the play park."

"You were so good to me, Abby…"

"But I did it for me, too. It helped, you know. It took the edge off my grief. It gave me something to focus on, and I loved being able to make you happy."

"I loved it, too," Laurel whispered. Which was why it had hurt so much when Abby walked away.

"But as the months and then the years went by, it felt like too much. I couldn't handle it all, and there was no support. I was doing my GCSEs, and then my A levels, and meanwhile I was basically raising you—giving you all your meals, helping you with your homework, washing your clothes. When I tried to get Dad more involved, he'd get angry with me. Not in an…an abusive way, but it still hurt. This was his job, and I was doing it for him."

"I'm sorry," Laurel said. She felt horribly guilty, for taking so much from Abby without ever truly realising it, at least at the time. "I made so much work for you…"

"It wasn't your fault, Laurel. You were a kid. I actually considered not going to uni so I could stay with you, or at least going somewhere local and living at home. Maybe I should have."

"You had to live your own life at some point." Laurel had never expected to justify Abby's actions to her, when they'd hurt so much at the time. But her sister had only been eighteen. Like she'd said, it hadn't been her job to raise Laurel.

"I told myself that thirteen was old enough."

"Almost as old as you were when Mum died."

"And that you'd be okay, and I'd come home on weekends, and maybe Dad would step up and this could all be a good thing."

"I can see that," Laurel said, and finally she *could*. She could see Abby's perspective—how trapped she must have felt, longing to finally live her own life, and yet beholden to Laurel. She'd been in an impossible situation, trying to make the best of it.

"But then I got to Sheffield..." Abby drew another ragged breath. "And it felt so wonderful, Laurel, like I could finally breathe. And everyone else there was so unbelievably free—they didn't have a *thing* to worry about. Clubbing every night and struggling to do their own laundry... they had no idea. But then I started to feel resentful. Bitter about how my life had turned out. And when I went home and saw how you were struggling to step into my shoes—making the meals, doing it all for him, I felt so guilty. And together, the guilt and the resentment, felt like this weight that I couldn't live under. I couldn't carry it."

"Oh, Abby," was all Laurel could say. It sounded so very awful.

"So I stayed away. And the more I stayed away, the more I justified it, and the harder and harsher I became. I'd backed myself into a corner and I tried not to care. And then I started on my career, and it felt so important to make something of myself, to justify all my choices all over again, and so I let work take up all my time and head space so then I didn't have to think about you or Dad or any of it."

"I'm sorry, for all of it." It felt like the only thing she could say.

"Laurel, don't be sorry." Abby sounded fierce. "None of this is your fault. You were just a kid. You didn't deserve any of it."

"Neither did you."

Abby shook her head. "I should have come back. When you were older, I could have explained something of what I'd been going through. But by then I felt too guilty and bitter and all the rest of it, and you'd stopped trying to reach out, and I let myself be angry about that because it was easier."

"Oh, Abby." A tear trickled down Laurel's cheek. "I wish we'd had this conversation so much sooner."

"I don't know if I could have." Abby took a sip of tea to steady herself. "I haven't been in a good place for a long time, Laurel. Working way too hard, fuelling myself with alcohol and painkillers. The Oxycodone started nearly ten years ago. And even before then... I've battled eating disorders, depression, you name it, I feel like I've had it. Why I thought I could be a good mother to Zac, I have no idea." She let out a wavering laugh as she shook her head.

"Zac is a great kid, Abby. That has to be down at least

somewhat to you."

"I got a message that he set fire to the chemistry lab?"

"It was a joke," Laurel protested, and then let out a little laugh, amazed that she was actually defending that particular misdemeanour. "Honestly, though. He's a good kid."

"I know he is, and I love him to bits." Abby shook her head. "I don't know if he believes that, but I do. Even though I've been a workaholic mother who offloaded him to day care when he was only three months old."

"Plenty of mums—"

"I went into it thinking I could finally get it right this time. I wanted a do over. This time I wouldn't just walk away, and yet look where I am now."

"But you weren't my mum," Laurel reminded her softly. "You're only six years older than me. You should have never been put in that role."

Abby made a face. "Tell that to Dad."

"Have you ever?" Laurel asked, and Abby jerked upright in surprise.

"What—"

"When's the last time you've spoken to him?"

She shook her head. "I don't even know. Twenty years ago, at least."

"That long?" Even though she knew their relationship had been fraught, Laurel hadn't realised it was as bad as that. She'd at least talked to her sister over the years, if very sporadically.

"Not since uni."

"And did you ever have it out? I mean, about how he left

you to it?"

"No, not really. Not at all. I made a few comments back at the beginning, and he'd grumble that he had a lot of work, that he wasn't good at that kind of stuff, whatever. I stopped trying."

"Maybe you need to talk to him," Laurel suggested. "Tell him how you've felt. Have some closure, if nothing else."

"I can't." Abby looked stricken. "I wouldn't even... I feel so guilty, Laurel. Still."

"Maybe it would help."

"You didn't turn bitter," Abby burst out. "You were left alone with him when you were just twelve. You had to do all the cooking and washing and the rest of it like I did. Why did you turn out so well?" She let out a wobbly laugh. "While I'm a basket case?"

"I don't know if I turned out well or not," Laurel admitted. She certainly had issues about commitment, which she hadn't even realised until recently. Until Archie. "But, in any case, I didn't have it nearly as hard as you did. I didn't have a little sister to take care of, after all. Dad and I had loads of takeaways, and he did his own washing. We just sort of rubbed along together, really."

Abby shook her head, a slow back and forth. "I wouldn't even know what to say to him now."

"But you could try," Laurel persisted. "It really might help, and even if it didn't, at least you'd made the effort. And Zac could meet his grandfather."

"After all this time..."

"A little road trip," Laurel encouraged. She felt, deep

down, that it was the right thing to do. That Abby wouldn't feel truly at peace until she'd confronted their father, until she'd confessed her guilt and then let it all go. "We could all go together, if you like. I haven't been back to Scarborough in a while, and I only live an hour away!"

"Don't you want to get back home to York?"

"Not really," Laurel admitted. She was surprised at how unwelcome the thought of her cosy cottage and old life was now. It all felt like a pale imitation of the real thing—a cluttered farmhouse in Orkney. A half-barmy sheep farmer with the loveliest eyes in the world.

"Why don't you?" Abby frowned and then leaned forward as if she could peer into Laurel's soul. "What are you not telling me?"

"Nothing," Laurel said, so half-heartedly that Abby just made a scoffing noise. "Nothing much," she amended, and then, because she knew her sister would get it out of her eventually, and also because she wanted to tell somebody, she started at the beginning and told her everything about Archie.

"He sounds lovely," Abby said when she'd finally finished, sniffling and trying not to feel heartbroken all over again. "You could have moved to Orkney."

"After knowing someone for a *week*?"

"More like ten days."

"Still, it's a bit much, isn't it?" Laurel protested. She felt a bizarre need to justify her choice, a panic that she'd done the wrong thing. "It's not like he even suggested something like that. Besides, Orkney is the back of beyond. The edge of nowhere. Miles and miles from civilisation. The nearest Starbucks is over a hundred miles away."

"It's not nowhere if your heart is there," Abby pointed out, and Laurel let out a laugh.

"I never thought of you as a romantic."

"When it comes to other people's lives…"

"Archie made it pretty clear," Laurel said in a tone of dismal finality. She couldn't forget that. "In the end, it was just a kiss."

"Some kiss."

Laurel nodded morosely, and they sipped their drinks in silence for a few moments. "So," she finally asked, trying for an upbeat tone. "What about Scarborough?"

THEY LEFT THE next day. Zac was surprisingly amenable to another road trip, and Abby had been seized by an almost grim determination to see this through.

"I think you're right," she told Laurel. "I need to talk to him. To tell him things. And if he won't be honest with me, or doesn't care, then at least I've said what I needed to say."

It was Laurel who rang her dad and asked him if she could visit, not mentioning Abby at her sister's request.

"Of course you can, love," her dad answered, affable as always. "I don't mind."

Living only an hour away, Laurel had visited her father once a month or so, usually coming for dinner, a takeaway in front of the TV. She ended up giving the kitchen a good clean, hoovering the downstairs, and putting a load or three of wash on, because her father had never really learned how to keep house, even after eighteen years on his own. Sometimes she even braved cleaning the toilets.

They never spoke much, but the silence had felt comfortable, like something frayed and faded but still wearable. Laurel had long ago learned not to expect anything more from her father.

Now, as they drove up the M1 towards Scarborough, she wondered how that relationship, or lack of it, had affected her over the years. Her mum and Abby had given her a fear of abandonment and a terror of commitment, all without realising it until recently. Had her father given her a self-protecting determination to have low expectations? To choose dreams over reality, because they never disappointed? They just didn't come true.

Inevitably Laurel's thoughts moved to Archie. He'd had his fair share of hardship—his brother dying, his mother leaving, his father's illness. What had he learned? To fear being left, that it was safer on his own? Was that why he'd backed off so quickly? Should she have tried harder? Dared more?

Everyone had baggage, Laurel acknowledged, no matter what their background. The best they could do was learn how to carry it, distribute the weight. Eventually, perhaps, they'd be able to shuck at least some of it off. Was that what Abby was doing now? Could she do it?

The slightly shabby semi-detached house on a suburban street on the outskirts of Scarborough looked like it hadn't changed at all in thirty years. The cars in the drives were newer models, and a few houses had a brighter lick of paint, but other than that Laurel felt as if they were stepping back in time.

The feeling was even more pronounced when her father opened the door and they stepped into the little foyer with its cabbage rose wallpaper and cheap wooden furniture bought from MFI circa 1980.

"Hey, Dad." She smiled at him and did the sort of half-hug that they always did, but in the middle of returning it, her father stared slack-jawed at Abby, and then at Zac behind her.

"Hey." Abby smiled stiffly; she was practically vibrating with tension. "It's been a long time."

"Yes…"

"I want to talk to you, Dad." Abby's voice wobbled. "About… about when Mum died. And after."

"What…" Her father looked flummoxed. "After all this time?"

"Yes," Abby said firmly. "After all this time."

Laurel and Zac went for a stroll around the block while Abby talked to their father. Laurel knew she needed privacy, and she was grateful to escape the tension.

As they walked along the wintry streets, she bored Zac with a few anecdotes from her childhood before she turned to him seriously.

"This is all going to get better, you know, right?"

He hunched his shoulders. "Is it?"

"You and your mum have been through some tough

times, I know. But I really think things are changing—in her, and maybe in you, too." Laurel held up a hand to stop the disdainful snort she knew was coming. "I know that all sounds mega sappy, but it's true, Zac. Your mum loves you. I love you." She paused, surprised by that admission. "I didn't expect to, you know. You were a real pain in the backside to start with."

Zac cracked a tiny smile. "You were annoying."

"I was not!"

"Fluttering all around, trying to impress me, treating me like I was six. I mean, *Ludo*."

Laurel smacked him playfully on the shoulder. "All right, fine, I was annoying. But things are going to be better now. They might be hard for a while, but they'll be better. I really do believe that."

Zac shrugged and kept walking, but Laurel saw what she thought might be a smile quirk the barest corner of his mouth. "Yeah, whatever," he said. "Maybe."

When they finally braved coming back to the house, Abby was in the kitchen, wiping her eyes. Laurel's heart lurched, and then she saw her father was in the living room, doing the same thing.

"What..." she began, unsure what question to ask.

"It's okay," Abby said, still wiping. "We've talked. Dad's said some things... I've said some things. But I think it's going to be all right."

"Oh, Abby..."

"Laurel."

She whirled around to see her father shuffling into the

doorway, looking like an old man in a way he never had before. "Laurel, I should say this to you, too. A long time ago." He gave her a trembling smile, so different from his usual stoical expression. "I'm sorry."

"Oh, Dad…"

And then they were all hugging, all four of them, and it was ridiculous and wonderful and definitely awkward, and they all looked a bit self-conscious as they stepped back, because they'd never been a hugging kind of family, except perhaps they'd become one now, with a little practise and effort.

"Will you stay the night?" their dad asked, and Laurel and Abby exchanged looks. Laurel shrugged; it was Abby's call.

"Yes," Abby said, "For the night. But then we have somewhere to be."

Laurel didn't realise what she meant until they were getting ready to leave the next morning, after a full English fry up with her dad making the eggs, and all of them learning how to love one another again, with stumbling steps and stammered sentences, trying to do it properly this time. Abby had been rather quiet all morning, although not in a bad way, but now, as she slid into the driver's seat she gave Laurel a sudden, serious look.

Laurel's heart lurched even though she had no idea what her sister was going to say. "What is it?"

"It's two hundred and thirty-nine miles back to London," she said, and Laurel looked at her in confusion.

"Okay…"

"And five hundred and twenty-three miles to Orkney." Laurel's mouth opened but no words came out. Abby gave her a lopsided smile, her eyes sparkling. "What if we just kept driving?"

"You mean…"

"*Yes,* Mum!" Zac said, lurching forward from the back seat with a fist pump. "Yes, do it, Mum. *Do it.*"

Still grinning, Abby turned the ignition. As they drove off with their dad waving madly, Laurel waved back and then twisted to face her sister.

"You aren't serious…"

"I am. Are you?"

Laurel knew what she was asking. She could feel it in the way her heart thumped and her mind raced. Abby had taken so many risks—she'd been honest, open, heart-rendingly vulnerable with Laurel, with Zac, with their father. Could she be the same… with Archie?

"Keep driving," she said, and from the backseat Zac let out a whoop of victory.

Chapter Sixteen

THERE WAS A slight flaw to their plan, which was that it was New Year's Eve, and when they arrived in Scrabster at ten o'clock at night, there were no ferries running. Obviously.

"This isn't a problem," Abby announced airily. "I've been here before. There's a guy who hires his boat out. He gave me his mobile. We'll be fine."

"It's ten o'clock on New Year's Eve," Laurel reminded her, somewhat hysterically. She'd spent the last ten and a half hours of travel in a heightened, surreal state, hardly able to believe they were actually doing this. "Hogmanay," she added. "In Scotland. A big deal, you know?"

"I think you've timed your arrival perfectly," Abby said with an insouciant shrug. "If you're lucky, the fireworks will start right as you lock eyes with Archie."

"*Abby.*" Laurel could hardly believe how nonchalant her sister was acting about this all. As they'd driven into Scotland, she'd remarked that maybe they'd all move to Orkney.

"Wait, what?" Laurel had goggled at her. "You live in London—"

"I never liked it all that much, and I don't think Zac did,

either." Zac shook his head vigorously. "And for the amount of money I could get for my flat, we could buy something really nice, and have loads leftover besides."

"Abby, this might not even work out, you know?" Laurel definitely sounded hysterical then. "I mean, I barely know Archie…"

Abby considered this for a moment. "We'll rent to start."

"*Yes*, Mum," Zac enthused from the backseat.

Laurel let out a sound—part groan, part shriek, part wild, crazy laughter. What were they *doing*?

"The thing is, Laurel," she said more seriously, "if I've learned anything from the train wreck of the last ten years, it's that you can't spend your life holding back and wondering what if. Go all in, and if it blows up in your face, well, at least you did it, you know? You won't spend the next twenty years wondering what could have happened."

"Is that what I'm going to do?"

"Probably, if you don't find Archie and tell him how you feel."

"I can't believe we're doing this," Laurel muttered. She felt close to hyperventilating.

What would Archie even think when he saw her—all of them? Laurel showing up with her family in tow, declaring true love, or something edging towards it. This was *crazy*.

And yet somehow it was happening. Abby called the guy with the boat, and he agreed to ferry them over for a rather exorbitant fee, at least by Laurel's standards, but Abby didn't bat an eyelid.

The sea was amazingly placid, unlike her first ferry crossing, but Laurel's stomach churned all the more. What was she *doing*? What was she going to say?

By the time they arrived in Stromness, it was half past eleven, and the town was strung with lights and thronged with people ready to welcome the new year. They were on foot, as they'd had to leave the car, in Scrabster, and suddenly, finally, Laurel felt completely overwhelmed and stopped right there in the street.

"I can't do this."

"Laurel," Abby said. "You *are* doing it."

"What if he's not home?" Laurel said in a panic. "What if I can't find him?"

"He's somewhere," Abby told her. "We'll find him."

"What if I do find him?"

"Then tell him how you feel."

"How do I feel?"

"You haven't figured that out yet?" Abby turned to her, as no-nonsense as she'd been when Laurel had been little, and she'd been telling her to do her homework or eat her peas. "Laurel, you don't have to say anything that isn't true. Don't make this more than it is, and don't make it less. You aren't in love with him, you don't him well enough yet, but you know him well enough to take a shot at happiness, so here you are, lining it up."

"You make it sound so easy…"

"No, not easy. Crazy hard, with emphasis on the crazy. But worthwhile."

"This *is* crazy," Laurel muttered for about the twentieth time. "Utterly *mad*."

"Yep," Zac said cheerfully. "Wait, I think I see someone I know."

It seemed like everyone in Stromness was out on the streets. The pubs had all closed at eleven, and everyone was gathered in Graham Place, one of the town's main squares, to hear the bells ring in the new year. It was ten to eleven. Laurel searched the crowds for Archie, sensing that he must be here. Wanting him to be, and yet terrified that he was.

Should she head to his farmhouse? Keep searching the crowds? Or run back to the harbour, and jump in the first boat she saw?

And then she saw him, and felt as if everyone crowding around her fell away. She walked towards him on feet that felt as if they were separated from her body, her mind buzzing blankly as she kept on going, one step after another. The crowds, the noise, the cold, all of it disappeared and all she saw was Archie.

He was chatting to someone she didn't recognise, which wasn't really a surprise, but he was wearing her sky-blue jumper, and it made her smile. It made her *hope*.

She kept walking, and then she was in front of him, feeling as if her whole heart must be visible in her eyes, and he turned and saw her, and his mouth dropped open.

"Laurel... I thought you'd gone."

"I did. I left three days ago." Had it only been three days since she'd last been here? How many lifetimes could she live in the space of a few weeks?

His forehead crinkled. "What..."

"I came back." She let out a trembling laugh, feeling her

whole world teeter on this moment. "I've been to London, and then to Scarborough, and now I've come here." She gulped. "I came back because of you." Archie looked confused, and Laurel's heart lurched sickeningly. What if this was all a mistake? What if this wasn't at all what she wanted?

What if it really had just been a kiss?

But even if it was, Laurel knew she still had to try. To risk. As much for her sake, more for her sake, than for Archie's. To prove she could, to finally take a chance with her life. With her heart.

"It wasn't just a kiss for me, Archie," she said in a rush. Her voice was shaking. "Not even close. It was so much more."

He stared at her, his mouth gaping open, looking gormless and confused and wonderful. "You want Mr Darcy."

"What?"

"I watched that blooming film. Colin Firth." He practically spat the words. "I'm naught like him."

"Oh, you silly man," Laurel cried. "I don't want Colin Firth. He was just a fantasy—a foolish fantasy I held onto because the real thing scared me so much. And it still scares me, but now I want to take a risk. A chance... with you." She let out another trembling laugh. "I want *you*, Archie. That's why I'm here. I know we don't know each other all that well, and we need time to just... *be*, I suppose, and I'm not asking for a proposal or something ridiculous like that, but just a chance to try. To see. Because, like Abby said, I don't want to spend the next twenty years wondering what if." She straightened her shoulders and stared him straight in the eye, wishing she could tell what he thought, but his face, that lovely, craggy face, was completely inscrutable. "That is, if you'd be willing to. If you want to."

"With you in York and me in Orkney?"

"Well, no." Laurel let out a shaky laugh. "I rather thought I might move up here for a bit. If that isn't too... much. Too crazy."

"Too crazy?" Archie raised his shaggy eyebrows. "It's utterly mad."

"Is it?" Laurel said in a small voice. *Oh no...*

"Utterly mad, and utterly brilliant... if you really want to." He looked at her seriously as Laurel's heart thumped a hard, staccato beat. "I've been cursing myself a stupid, frightened fool for letting you go. Practically pushing you away. But I was scared, lass, I have to admit it. I was scared to admit how much I'd come to care about you, scared of being left again."

"I shouldn't have left. I didn't want to. I care about you, Archie."

They stared at each other with wide eyes as the kirk's bells began to ring.

"Oh, kiss her already, you great, bliddy fool," someone shouted, and Archie laughed, a question in his eyes. A question Laurel answered easily, wonderfully with her own look.

And then his arms were around her, and his lips were on hers, hard and soft, wonderful and right, and she knew she'd come home. To Orkney, to Archie. To everything.

"I would have come," Archie said as they broke apart. "If

you hadn't first. I would have come and found you. I was just working up the courage."

Laurel laid her hand against his cheek. "I know you would have," she said, because now she did.

And then they kissed again, as everyone around them cheered and the bells rang in the new year, with all of its hope and joy.

Epilogue

One year later

"THE POTATOES ARE burning!"

"I've got them, lass."

Archie slotted Laurel a loving, laughing look as he whisked them off the top of the Aga. Aon, or maybe Dha, or Tri—Laurel still couldn't tell them apart—sniffed hopefully at his feet.

It was Christmas Day, four months after their wedding at the kirk in Stromness, and they were having everyone over for dinner. Abby and Zac, who were living in Kirkwall, and Laurel's father, who had come up for the week from Scarborough. Archie's father was coming too, a day trip from his nursing home, and Eilidh had decided her joints could manage a winter in Orkney and would be walking across the paddock any moment.

The kitchen—and their hearts—were full.

It had been a wonderful, crazy, and sometimes difficult year, learning to live in Orkney, and falling in love with Archie. Laurel had moved to a rented cottage in Stromness with her cat Mistral, missing her friends back in York but knowing deep in her bones that she was doing the right thing. She and Archie had started dating, even if it had felt like they were miles beyond chitchat and movie nights.

Then, three months after Laurel had moved to Orkney, over dinner in Archie's cluttered kitchen, he'd laid down his fork and given her a serious look.

"I can't do this anymore, lass," he said, and Laurel had stared at him in disbelief and a little concern.

"What…"

"This dating business. I'm forty-five now, and you're thirty-six. We're too old for this."

"What… what are you suggesting?"

"Let's do it properly and get married. I know I want to marry you, and I hope you want to marry me. I want to start a real life together, not this faffing about." His expression softened. "And I want a bairn or two, if God wills it."

Laurel's heart had somersaulted as she'd let out a wobbly laugh. "Was that a proposal?"

Archie looked abashed. "Not very romantic, was it?"

"It was perfect." She threw her arms around him. "And very you. The answer is yes."

They picked out a ring in Kirkwall the next day, a local piece of twisted silver and freshwater pearls. And they started planning their wedding, a community celebration, a joyous occasion that was everything Laurel had wanted and more.

Over the last year she'd got firmly involved in the small Orkney community—knitting circle, book club, food bank volunteer, church member, Archie's wife. She'd made friends, and she'd travelled to York a few times to visit her old ones, and over the last four months Mistral had learned to tolerate Aon, Dha, and Tri, who, rather inexplicably, treated the cat like a little sister.

And now Christmas. The best Christmas yet, with stockings full of treats by the fire in the sitting room, and a roast turkey glistening on the kitchen table, nearly bowed under the weight of all the food.

"Anyone home?" Eilidh called as she opened the kitchen door, and Laurel hurried to greet her.

"Aunt Eilidh! I'm so glad you came."

"And I'm so glad you came," Eilidh answered with a twinkle in her eye. "A year ago."

Archie laughed as he put his arm around Laurel's shoulders. "Not as glad as I am."

"No, definitely not."

"We're here," Abby announced, as she came in with Zac, Tom West following behind. He was spending the week at Abby's house, insisting the newlyweds needed their space, although Laurel suspected it was more that her father wanted to spend time with his oldest daughter.

Archie went to bring his dad, who had been dozing by the fire, into the kitchen, and a few chaotic minutes later, they all sat down to eat, the table wonderfully crowded.

Sitting at one end, with Archie at the other, Laurel met his eyes and smiled. She was so happy, and so very thankful.

Miracles really did happen, she knew now. She just had to believe… and then see.

And she knew both she and Archie saw the miracle, the magic, as everyone linked hands and her husband began to say grace.

The End

If you enjoyed Christmas at the Edge of the World, why not try one of Kate's other books, such as the Willoughby Close or Holley Sisters series?

If you enjoyed this book, please leave a review at your favorite online retailer! Even if it's just a sentence or two it makes all the difference.

Thanks for reading *Christmas at the Edge of the World* by Kate Hewitt!

Discover your next romance at TulePublishing.com.

TULE
PUBLISHING

More books by Kate Hewitt

The Willoughby Close series

Book 1: *A Cotswold Christmas*

Book 2: *Meet Me at Willoughby Close*

Book 3: *Find Me at Willoughby Close*

Book 4: *Kiss Me at Willoughby Close*

Book 5: *Marry Me at Willoughby Close*

Available now at your favorite online retailer!

The Holley Sisters of Thornthwaite series

Book 1: *A Vicarage Christmas*

Book 2: *A Vicarage Reunion*

Book 3: *A Vicarage Wedding*

Book 4: *A Vicarage Homecoming*

Available now at your favorite online retailer!

If you enjoyed *Christmas at the Edge of the World*, you'll love these other Tule Christmas books!

A Christmas Romance
by Nancy Holland

Christmas with the Firefighter
by Clare Connelly

Long Lost Christmas
by Joan Kilby

Available now at your favorite online retailer!

About the Author

After spending three years as a diehard New Yorker, **Kate Hewitt** now lives in the Lake District in England with her husband, their five children, and a Golden Retriever. She enjoys such novel things as long country walks and chatting with people in the street, and her children love the freedom of village life—although she often has to ring four or five people to figure out where they've gone off to.

She writes women's fiction as well as contemporary romance under the name Kate Hewitt, and whatever the genre she enjoys delivering a compelling and intensely emotional story.

Thank you for reading

Christmas at the Edge of the World

If you enjoyed this book, you can find more from all our great authors at TulePublishing.com, or from your favorite online retailer.

TULE
PUBLISHING

Made in the USA
Monee, IL
22 January 2021